Also by William Maxwell

SO LONG, SEE YOU TOMORROW   *1980*

OVER BY THE RIVER   *1977*

ANCESTORS   *1971*

THE CHATEAU   *1961*

STORIES *(with Jean Stafford,*
John Cheever, and Daniel Fuchs)   *1956*

TIME WILL DARKEN IT   *1948*

THE HEAVENLY TENANTS   *1946*

THE FOLDED LEAF   *1945*

THEY CAME LIKE SWALLOWS   *1937*

BRIGHT CENTER OF HEAVEN   *1934*

The Old Man at the Railroad Crossing

and Other Tales

William Maxwell

The Old Man at
the Railroad Crossing
and Other Tales

NONPAREIL BOOKS
David R. Godine, Publisher
BOSTON

This is a *Nonpareil Book* published in 1987 by
DAVID R. GODINE, PUBLISHER, INC.
Horticultural Hall
300 Massachusetts Avenue
Boston, Massachusetts 02115

Library of Congress Cataloging in Publication Data
Maxwell, William, 1908–
The old man at the railroad crossing and other tales.
(Nonpareil books ; 45)
I. Title. II. Series: Nonpareil book ; 45.
PS3525.A946404 1987   813'.54   86-46248
ISBN 0-87923-676-0

First printing

Printed in the United States of America

For Em
because, on her birthday, something needed to be said, objects are not enough, and you cannot wrap up a summer night, a cloud, the falling snow, a star, or a western pine tree.

Note

THESE twenty-nine tales were written over a period of
many years, usually for an occasion, and I didn't so
much write them as do my best to keep out of the way of
their writing themselves. I would sit with my head bent
over the typewriter waiting to see what was going to
come out of it. The first sentence was usually a surprise
to me. From the first sentence everything else followed. A
person I didn't know anything about and had never known
in real life—a man who had no enemies, a girl who doesn't
know whether to listen to her heart or her mind, a woman
who never draws breath except to complain, an old man
afraid of falling—stepped from the wings and began to act
out something I must not interrupt or interfere with, but
only be a witness to: a life, with the fleeting illuminations
that anybody's life offers, written in sand with a pointed
stick and erased by the next high tide. In sequence the tales
seem to complement one another. There are recurring
themes. But I did not plan it that way. I have sometimes
believed that it was all merely the result of the initial waiting with an emptied mind—that this opened a door of some
kind, and what emerged was an archaic survival, the pro-

fessional storyteller who flourished in all the countries of the world before there were any printed books, a dealer in the unexpected turn of events, in the sudden reversal of fortune that changes a human being's fate; old, frail, led around by a young boy, his voice now gentle as a dove, now implacable, as he approaches the moment of irony; half-blind, but having seen such wonders as will require all his talent to tell about, and the emotional participation of whoever stops to listen to him.

Contents

1	The man who had no enemies	3
2	The blue finch of Arabia	10
3	The girl with a willing heart and a cold mind	16
4	The poor orphan girl	20
5	The country where nobody ever grew old and died	27
6	The woman who lived beside a running stream	32
7	The marble watch	39
8	The half-crazy woman	47
9	The two women friends	50
10	The fisherman who had no one to go out in his boat with him	56
11	The carpenter	62
12	The man who lost his father	68
13	The industrious tailor	73
14	The woman with a talent for talking	84
15	The man who took his family to the seashore	90
16	The woman who didn't want anything more	95
17	The kingdom where straightforward, logical thinking was admired over every other kind	101
18	The woman who had no eye for small details	112
19	The woodcutter	119

20 The shepherd's wife   125
21 The man who loved to eat   131
22 The epistolarian   135
23 The problem child   140
24 The printing office   147
25 The lamplighter   153
26 The old man who was afraid of falling   158
27 The man who had never been sick a day in his
      life   163
28 The woman who never drew breath except to
      complain   166
29 The old man at the railroad crossing   171

The Old Man at
the Railroad Crossing
and Other Tales

I

The man who had no enemies

O NCE upon a time there was a man who had no enemies —only friends. He had a gift for friendship. When he met someone for the first time, he would look into the man or the woman or the child's eyes, and he never afterward mistook them for someone else. He was as kind as the day is long, and no one imposed on his kindness. He had a beautiful wife, who loved him. He had a comfortable, quiet apartment in town and a beautiful little house by the sea. He had enough money. All summer he taught children to sail boats on the salt water, and on winter afternoons he sat in his club and helped old men with one foot in the grave to remember names, so they could get on with their recollecting. If necessary, he even helped them to remember the point of the recollection, which he had usually heard before. In the club he was never alone for a minute. If he sat down by the magazine table, the other members gathered around him like fruit flies—the young, uneasy new members as well as his bald-headed contemporaries. The places he had lived in stretched halfway around the world, and he was a natural born storyteller. His conversation went to the head, like wine. At the same time, it went straight to the heart. He was a lovely man, and there aren't any more like him.

But there was also in the same club a man who had no friends—and, of course, not a single enemy either. He was always alone. He had never married. Though he had too much money, no one had ever successfully put the finger on him. He did not drink, and if someone who had been drinking maybe a little too much nodded to him on the way upstairs to the dining room, he did not respond, lest it turn out that he had been mistaken for somebody else. He tried sitting at the common table, in the hope that it would broaden his mind, but it was not the way he had been given to understand it would be, so he moved to a table by the window, a table for two, and for company he had an empty plate that did not contradict itself, a clean napkin that lived wholly in the present, a glittering glass tumbler that had its facts and figures straight, an unprejudiced knife, an unsentimental fork, and two logical spoons. Actually, his belonging to this particular club at all was due to a mistake on the part of the secretary of the committee on admissions, who had been instructed to notify another man of the same name that he had been elected to membership.

The man who had no friends did not want any, but he was observing, and from his table by the window he saw something no one else saw: The man who had no enemies, only friends, did not look well. It could be nothing more than one of those sudden jerks by which people grow older, but there was a late-afternoon light in his eye, and also his color was not good. Joking, he made use of the elevator when the others moved toward the stairs. And more and more he seemed like a man who is listening to two conversations at once. Sometimes for a week or ten days he would not appear at the club at all, and then he would be there again, moving through the stately, high-ceilinged rooms like a ship under full sail—but a ship whose rigging is frayed and whose oak timbers have grown lighter and lighter with time, and whose seaworthiness is now entirely a matter of the excellence of the builder's design.

The first stroke was slight. The doctor kept him in bed for a while, but he was able to spend the summer in his house by the sea, as usual. During the period of his convalescence, his wife informed the doorman at the club that he would be happy to see his friends. Naturally, they came —came often, came in droves, and found the invalid sitting up in bed, in good spirits, though not quite his old self yet. They were concerned lest they stay too long, and at the same time found it difficult to leave until they had blurted out, while it was still possible, how much he meant to them. These statements he was somehow able to dispose of with humor, so that they didn't hang heavy in the air afterward.

The man who had no friends also inquired about him, and the doorman, after some hesitation, gave him the message too, thinking that since this was the first time in fourteen years that he had ever asked about anybody, he must be a friend. But he didn't pay a call on the sick man. He had asked only out of curiosity. When he returned to town in September, he saw on the club bulletin board an announcement of a memorial service for the man who had a gift for friendship. He had died about a month before, in his sleep, in the house by the sea. The man who had no friends had reached the age where it is not unusual to spend a considerable part of one's time going to funerals, but no one had died whose obsequies required his presence, and again he was curious. He marked the date in the little memorandum book he always carried with him, and when the day came he got in a taxi and went to the service.

THE small stone chapel filled up quickly, for of course they all came, all the friends of the man who had no enemies. They came bringing their entire stock of memories of him, which in one or two instances went back to their early youth. And in many cases there was something about their dress, some small mark of color—the degree of red or bright blue that is permitted in the ties of elderly men, the *Légion d'honneur* in a lapel—because it had seemed to them that the occasion ought not to be wholly solemn, since the man himself had been so impatient of solemnity. The exception was the man who had no friends. He wore a dark gray business suit and a black-and-white striped tie, and sat alone in the back of the chapel. To his surprise, the funeral service was completely impersonal. Far from eulogizing the dead man or explaining his character to people who already knew all there was to know about it, the officiating clergyman did not even mention his name. There was a longish prayer, and then quotations from the Scriptures—mostly from the Psalms. The chapel had a bad echo, but the idea of the finality of death came through the garbled phrases, even so. The idea of farewell. The idea of a funeral on the water, and mourners peering, through torchlight, at a barque that is fast disappearing from sight. The man who had no friends sat observing, with his inward eye, his own funeral, in an empty undertaking parlor. The church was cold. He felt a draft on his ankles.

The young minister raised his voice to that pitch that is customary when the prayers of clergymen are meant to carry not only to the congregation but also to the ear of Heaven. There was a last brief exhortation to the Deity, and then the service was over. But during the emptying of the chapel something odd happened. The people there had not expected to derive such comfort from the presence of one another, and when their eyes met, their faces lit up, and they kept reaching out their hands to each other, over the pews. The man who had no friends saw what was happening and hurriedly put on his overcoat, but before he could slip out of the church, he felt his arm being taken in a friendly manner, and a man he knew only by sight said, "Ah yes, he belonged to you too, didn't he? Yes, of course." And no sooner had he extricated himself from this person than someone else said, "You're not going off by yourself? Come with us. Come on, come on, stop making a fuss!" And though he could hardly believe it, he found himself sitting on the jump seat of a taxi, with four other men, who took out their handkerchiefs and unashamedly wiped the tears away, blew their noses, and then sat back and began to tell funny stories about the dead man. When he got out of the cab, he tried to pay for his share, but they wouldn't hear of it, so he thanked them stiffly, and they called goodbye to him as if they were all his friends, which was too absurd—except that it didn't end there. The next day at the club they went right on acting as if they had a right to consider themselves his friends, and nothing he said or didn't say made any difference. They had got it into their heads he was a friend of the man who died, and so one of them. Shortly after the beginning of the new year, what should he find but a letter, on club stationery, informing him that he had been elected to the Board of Governors. He sat right down and wrote a letter explaining why he could not serve, but he saw at once that the letter was too revealing, so he tore it up. For the next three years he went faithfully, but with no pleasure, to the monthly dinners, and cast his vote with the others during the business meeting that followed the dinner. At the very last meeting of his term, just when he thought he was escaping, the secretary read off the names of the members who were to serve on the House Committee, and his name was among them. It seemed neither the time nor the place to protest, and afterward, when he did protest, he was told that it was customary for the members of the Board of Governors to serve on one committee or another after their term was finished. If he refused, the matter would be placed before the Board of Governors at their next meeting. He didn't want to call that much attention to himself, so he gave in. He served on the House Committee for two years, and at these meetings found that he was in sympathy with the prevailing atmosphere, which was of sharp candor and common sense. Inevitably he became better acquainted with his fellow committee members, and when they spoke to him on the stairs he couldn't very well not respond. For a while he continued to sit at his table by the window, but someone almost always came and joined him, so in the end he decided he might as well move over to the common table with the others. Later he served on the Rules Committee, the Archives Committee, the Art Committee, the Library Committee, the Music Committee, and the Committee on Admissions. Finally, when there were no more committees for him to serve on, someone dropped a remark in his presence and he saw the pit yawning before him. He took a solemn vow that he would never permit his name to be put up for president of the club, but it was put up; they did it without asking his permission, for it was an honor that had never been refused and they couldn't imagine anyone's wanting to refuse it.

He made an ideal president. He understood facts and

figures, being a man of means, and since he had no family life, he was free to give all his time to the affairs of the club. A curmudgeon with a heart of gold is what they all said about him. Sometimes they even said it to his face. Fuming, he was made to sit for his portrait, shortly before he died, at the age of eighty-four, of pneumonia. As so often happens, the portrait was a failure. There was a bleak look in the eyes that wasn't at all like him, the members said, shaking their heads, and the one man who really understood him—who had never once tried to be his friend—was not there to contradict them.

2

The blue finch of Arabia

AFTER dark on the evening of the twenty-fourth of
December, an old woman and an old man got off the
train at a little wayside station on the Trans-Siberian Railroad and hurried across the snow to the only lighted shop
in the village, which was a pet shop. In their excitement
they left the door open, which annoyed the proprietor, who
was deaf, and they had a hard time making him understand
what they wanted. They had come from Venice, they
said, on the strength of a rumor that he had a pair of blue
finches. The proprietor shook his head. He had had *one*
blue finch, not a pair, and he had sold it that morning.

"Tell us who you sold it to!" the old woman cried.

"We'll give you a thousand dollars," the old man said,
"if you'll just tell us his name."

"I didn't ask him."

"But how could you *not* ask him his name?" the old
man and the old woman cried.

"Did I ask yours when you came in just now and left the
door wide open?" the proprietor said. "Besides, it was the
common blue finch of Africa, and not the one you are
looking for."

"You know about the blue finch of Arabia?" the old man shouted.

"Certainly," said the pet-shop proprietor.

"But I daresay you have never seen one?" said the old woman slyly, in a normal tone of voice, hoping to test the pet-shop proprietor's hearing.

"A pair only," the proprietor said, turning off his hearing aid. "Never just one."

"We'll give you two thousand dollars," said the old man, dancing up and down, "if you'll just tell us where you saw them."

"Very well," said the pet-shop proprietor. "Where is the two thousand?"

"What's that?" asked the old man.

"I say where is the two thousand dollars?" the pet-shop proprietor shouted. "This is a very good hearing aid I am wearing. Here—try it, why don't you?"

The old man looked at the old woman, who nodded, and then he reached in his pocket and took out his checkbook, and she opened her purse and took out her pen, and then he turned to the pet-shop proprietor. "Name?" he shouted.

"Make it out to cash," the pet-shop proprietor said.

When the old man had finished writing out the check for two thousand dollars, he put it on the counter between the pet-shop proprietor and him, and he and the old woman leaned forward with their eyes bright and their mouths open and said, "Now, tell us where you saw them. They're worth half a million dollars."

"The pair of blue finches?"

"Are we talking about canaries?" asked the old man, drumming his nails on the counter.

"I saw them—" the pet-shop proprietor said, closing his eyes; "I saw them—" he repeated, looking tired and ill, and older than he had looked when they first came into the shop; "I saw them—" he said, suddenly opening his eyes and looking happier than the old man and the old woman had ever seen anybody look, *"in a forest in Arabia."*

The old man shrieked with anger and disappointment, and the old woman reached for the check for two thousand dollars, which was already in the pet-shop proprietor's wallet in his inside coat pocket, though nobody saw him pick it up, fold it, and put it there.

The old man and the old woman ran out into the deep snow, crying police, crying help, and leaving the door wide open behind them. As it happened, there were no police at that wayside station on the Trans-Siberian Railroad. They rattled the door of the railway station but it was locked. On the outside, the schedule of trains was posted, and they lit matches, which they shielded with their hands and then with the old man's hat, trying to make out how long they would have to wait in the cold before another train came along that would take them back to Venice. When they did see, finally, they couldn't believe it, and went on lighting more matches and looking at the timetable in despair. The next train going in either direction was due in nine days. In the end, since all the other houses were closed and dark, they had to go back to the pet shop, and this time the old man pulled the door to after him. The pet-shop proprietor, seeing that they were about to speak, adjusted his hearing aid; but though they opened their mouths again and again, no sound came out, and after shaking the apparatus several times, the pet-shop proprietor put it in his pocket and said in a normal tone of voice, "If you don't mind the conversation of birds, and if fish don't make you restless, and if you like cats and don't have fleas, there is no reason why you can't stay here until your train comes."

So they did. They stayed nine days, there in the pet shop, among the birds of every size and color, and the cats of all description, the monkeys and the dogs, the long-tailed goldfish, and the tame raccoons. At first they were restless, but they had promised not to be, and gradually, because whatever the pet-shop proprietor did was interesting and whatever he had in his shop was living and beautiful, they forgot about themselves, about the passing of time, about Venice, where they had a number of important appointments that it would cost them money not to keep, and even about the blue finch of Arabia, which they had never seen but only heard about. What they had heard was how rare and valuable it was, not that its song is more delicate than gold wire and its least movement like the reflections of water on a wall. The old woman helped the pet-shop proprietor clean out the cages, and the old man brushed and curried the cats, who soon grew very attached to him, and when the pet-shop proprietor said suddenly, "You have just time to walk from here to the railway station at a reasonable pace before your train pulls in," they were shocked and horrified.

"But can't we stay?" the old woman cried. "We've been so happy here these last nine days."

The pet-shop proprietor shrugged his shoulders. "It's all right with me if you want to spend the rest of your life in a wayside station on the Trans-Siberian Railroad," he said, "but what about the appointments you have in Venice?"

The old woman looked at the old man, who nodded sadly.

"Before you go," said the pet-shop proprietor, "I would like to present you with a souvenir of the establishment."

He opened a wire door just large enough to put his hand through, and reached into a huge cage that went all the way up to the ceiling and the whole length of the room and was full of birds of every size and color, and took out two small ones, both of them blue as the beginning of the night when there is deep snow on the ground. "Here," he said, thrusting the birds into a little wire cage and closing the door on them.

"But won't they get cold?" the old woman asked. "Won't they die on that long train ride?"

"Why should they?" asked the pet-shop proprietor. "They came all the way from—"

At that moment they heard the train whistle, the train that was taking them back to Venice, and so the old man rushed for the door, and the old woman picked up the cage with the blue birds in it and put it under her coat, and they floundered through the snow to the railway station, and the conductor pulled them up onto the train, which was already moving, and it was just as the pet-shop proprietor said: the birds stood the journey better than the old man and the old woman.

At the border the customs inspector boarded the train, and went through everybody's luggage until he came to the old man and the old woman, who were dozing. He shook first one and then the other, and pointing to the bird cage he said, "What kind of birds are those?"

"Bluebirds," the old man said, and shut his eyes.

"They look to me like the blue finch of Arabia," the customs inspector said. "Are you sure they're bluebirds?"

"Positive," the old woman said. "A man who has a pet shop in a wayside station of the Trans-Siberian Railroad gave them to us, so we don't have to pay duty on them. The week before, he sold somebody a blue finch, but it was the common blue finch of Africa."

"We had all that long trip there," the old man said, opening one eye, "and this long trip back, for nothing. When do we get to Venice?"

"If they had been the blue finch of Arabia," the customs inspector said, "you would have been allowed to keep them. Ordinary birds can't cross the border.

"But they do all the time," the old woman said, "in the sky."

"I know," the customs inspector said, "but not on the Trans-Siberian Railroad. Hand me the cage, please."

The old man looked at the old woman, who stood up stiffly, from having been in one position so long, and together they got off the train, missing their appointments in Venice, and spent the remaining years of their life in a foreign country, rather than part with a pair of birds that they had grown attached to on a long train journey, because of their color, which was as blue as the beginning of night when there is deep snow on the ground, and their song, which was more delicate than gold wire, and their movements, which were like the reflections of water on a wall.

3

The girl with a willing heart
and a cold mind

Nᴏᴛ everybody's heart and mind reside in their body.
There was a girl whose feelings and ideas led so
separate a life that they were to her always like a younger
brother and sister whom she cared for anxiously, as if
they had to be watched, and might, the moment she turned
her back, fall and skin their knees, or wander, picking
flowers, too close to the edge of some terrible cliff. When
she fell in love with a young fisherman who went out
every day, whether it was storming or fine weather, with
five other men in a sturdy boat, and came in the evenings
to sit beside her on her father's doorstep and plead with
her to marry him, she consulted both her heart and her
mind, for she didn't want to leave them behind when she
went to live with the fisherman, and she didn't want them
to be unhappy. Her heart was willing. It said, "Oh, let
us go and live with the fisherman and keep his house clean
and the fire burning all day on his hearth and have a good
supper waiting for him when he comes home at the end of
the day, half frozen with the cold. Let us go, by all means.
The fisherman needs us. The very sound of his voice plead-

ing is more than I can bear." But her mind was skeptical. It would not take a stand, not believing in one thing more than another.

After the girl and the young fisherman were married, and the girl kept his house clean for him and the fire burning brightly on the hearth and the kettle ready to boil the moment he came in at night, her mind gave them no peace. First it set upon the fisherman, who was a simple creature, not used to doubting, and when he drew the girl on his lap after supper, her mind came between them and said "Do you really love her, fisherman, or are you only pretending?" until the poor man grew vague and absentminded in his answers and sought comfort in sleep. Then her mind, not being at all satisfied with this small triumph, plagued and pestered the girl. When the fisherman lifted her in his arms and carried her off to bed, her mind said, "Why are you here? How did it ever come about? Weren't you happier before, in your father's house, sleeping in your own narrow cot? Wasn't that what you really wanted?" And the poor girl, not being able to answer, lay awake hour after hour, listening to the sound of the fisherman's heavy breathing by her side. Her only comfort at such times was her heart, with its steady beating.

"Heart, are you there?" the poor girl would ask. "Heart, do you feel anything?"

"Yes, I feel something," her heart told her patiently. "Go to sleep. It's only your mind filling you with doubts. In the morning, in broad daylight, everything will be all right. Have trust in me."

And finally, out of weariness, the girl fell asleep. But even with the fisherman's arm around her, and his heart beating against her ribs, she had troubled dreams and cried out unintelligibly in her sleep and woke up exhausted in the cold morning light. The color left her cheeks and she grew thinner, and the fisherman quarrelled with the other men, his boat companions, and cut himself with his knife because his hands were unsteady, and neglected to mend his nets, so that the best fish sometimes got away. And when he got home at night, the fire on the hearth had gone out, the house was dark, and no voice answered his call, and he had to go wandering off over the moors, tired though he was, until he found his wife, her hair damp with mist and her lips tasting of salt spray, and a lost look in her great dark eyes.

If he didn't come back, the girl thought, walking home with him hand in hand—if some night it got dark and I were waiting with supper all ready on the hearth and I didn't hear his step outside but only the wind howling and the branches scraping against the window and no sound indoors but the ticking of the clock, and if I put on a shawl finally and went outside and found the other women waiting on the cliff, their faces stiff with fright, their eyes intent on the darkness, and no boat on the sand, then I would know beyond all doubt whether I loved him or not. Then I would know if my heart is feeling. And when her husband, noticing her silence, asked her what she was thinking about, she shook her head or told him some small lie: she was worrying about the peas, which had a burnt taste because the water had all boiled off while she was getting wood for the fire, or about the postman's little girl, who had rheumatic fever. But actually it was his own face that she was thinking of, when they brought him in, lifeless, his hair matted and wet, and laid his body across the bed—his beautiful, loving, dead face.

And when he suddenly gave up going out in the early morning with the men in their boat, and took a job with the peat cutters and came home at night smelling of the marsh grass instead of the sea, she felt that there was no hope of her ever being happy, no way that she would ever know whether she loved him or not. And things might have gone on this way all her life if her body, which had no traffic with either her heart or her mind, hadn't rebelled finally and said, "You silly girl, I will now show you. I will give you an answer that you can't argue yourself out of. You are already with child, do you understand? The fisherman's child is growing inside of you, and has the fisherman's eyes and hair and his patient, loving disposition. You can go home to your father now or you can stay with the fisherman. Now is the time to decide."

The voice of her body was so stern and uncompromising that the girl began to weep. "O mind," she cried, "what are you thinking? O heart, what are you feeling now?"

There was no answer. She thought for a moment that both mind and heart had deserted her and that she was a madwoman. But then she put her hand to her side and felt her heart beating there, like her husband's heart inside his rising and falling chest, and her thoughts came now from her head, not from outside her. She threw her arms around the fisherman so wildly that he woke and made a warm nest for her in the curve of his naked body.

"Go to sleep," he said. "You've been dreaming. You've had a bad dream. While I'm here, no harm shall touch you." She smiled in the dark at his childish pride and thinking about the child inside her, which had his sea-blue eyes and his clustering dark hair, she fell into a dreamless sleep.

When he woke in the morning and put out his hand, she was gone. His heart beat in terror until he heard her moving about in the next room, setting the table for breakfast, and singing softly so as not to wake him.

4

The poor orphan girl

O NCE upon a time there was a poor orphan girl who had no mother and no father and was raised by her grandmother on one of the wind-swept islands of the Outer Hebrides. When she began running after the boys, her grandmother shipped her off to a cousin in Glasgow. At first the girl was well behaved and lent a hand wherever it was needed, and the cousin thought the grandmother just didn't understand the younger generation. But then she started staying out late at night and keeping bad company, and the cousin saw what the grandmother was up against. So she had a serious talk with the girl, and the girl made all sorts of promises, which she didn't keep, and the cousin didn't want to be blamed if the girl got in the family way, so she took her to an employment agency that specialized in sending servants to America.

"Mercy!" exclaimed the head of the most dependable domestic employment agency in New York City, when she looked at the girl's folder. "An unspoiled country girl, willing and strong, and with a heart of gold!" The folder was shown to a Class A client with a Fifth Avenue address, who snapped her up. The immigration papers were filled out, and the deposit paid, and the girl found herself on a boat going to America. What she was expecting was, naturally, what she had seen in the flicks. What she got was a six-by-eleven bedroom looking out on the back of another building, with a closet six inches deep, and the customary dwarf's bathtub that you find in servants' bathrooms in old apartment buildings. On the other hand, the girl had never before had a bed all to herself and a toilet that wasn't either outdoors or on the landing and shared by several large families. She wrote home to her grandmother that she was in luck.

She got on all right with the cook, and there was no heavy work, because a cleaning woman came in twice a week and a laundress two days, and the windows were done by a window-washing company, and all the girl had to do was remember what she was told. Unfortunately, this was more than she could manage. During dinner parties she couldn't decide whether you serve from the right and clear from the left or serve from the left and clear from the right, so she did both, and when she made the beds the top sheet was not securely fastened, and she used the master's washcloth to clean the tub, and what with one thing and another, including the state of her room, she received notice after two weeks and returned to the employment office looking only a little less fresh than when she arrived from Scotland. The head of the agency said, "This time suppose we don't aim quite so high. You don't mind children?" The girl said no, she liked children—which was true, she did—and off she went to an address on Park Avenue. The interview was successful, and she found herself in the exact same bedroom with the shallow closet and the little bath, only the room looked out on a blank wall instead of the back of another building. The work was harder than before and the hours much longer, but at least there were no dinner parties. She was supposed to have breakfast ready by quarter of eight, which was impossible, but she tried. Then she walked the children to the corner where they took the school bus, and made the children's beds, and picked up the toys, and ran the vacuum, and stuffed the clothes into the washing machine and the dryer, and so on.

In the afternoon, she walked the dog and went to the supermarket, where she soon knew everybody, and Joe, who weighed the vegetables and was old enough to be her father, said, "Here comes my sweetheart," and Arthur the butcher said, "Tell me—where'd you get those beautyful eyes?" Then she took the children to the Park, and got their supper, and so on. She was supposed to baby-sit when the master and mistress went out, but they didn't very often go out. Once in a blue moon, to an early movie, was about the extent of it. If she had been in Glasgow, she would have known what to do with her evenings. Here she didn't know anybody, so she went to bed.

ONE day when she was with the children in the Park, she met a girl named Cathleen, who asked her to go with her to a dance hall on Eighty-sixth Street. This turned out to be very different from the Outer Hebrides, and just like the flicks. The next morning, her head was full of impressions, mostly of a sad young man who said he was in love with her and almost persuaded her to go home with him, and she was simultaneously pleased with herself for resisting temptation and sorry she hadn't done it. She burned the bacon, and the master wrinkled his nose over the coffee, but by that time she was stretched out on her bed getting forty winks. As the day wore on, a number of things went wrong: the dishwasher foamed all over the kitchen floor, because she had used the washing-machine detergent, and she broke a cup, and put a pair of red corduroy overalls in the washing machine in the same load with some pillowcases and the mistress's blouses and the children's underwear. They all were stained a permanent pink, but the mistress forgave her, because anyone can make a mistake now and then, and the cup was too small a matter to make a thing of. During dinner, the telephone rang, and it was for her. Though she had intended to fall into bed as soon as she finished the dinner dishes, she got dressed instead and met Cathleen at a bar on Second Avenue, where they fed dimes into a jukebox, and another boy wanted her to go home with him, and she was so tired she almost did, but instead she left before Cathleen was ready, and was home in bed by two o'clock. She overslept, and there wasn't even time to comb her hair. She managed to stay out of sight until the master had left for his office, but then she forgot, so the mistress did catch her looking like I don't know what. A queer expression passed over her face, but she didn't say anything, and the girl realized that the mistress wasn't ever going to say anything *no matter what happened.*

The telephone always seemed to ring during dinner, and though there was an extension in the kitchen, the girl didn't think it was polite for her to answer it, so she let the master get up from the table and go to the phone in the bedroom. Sometimes, after the third or fourth call, she thought she could detect a note of irritation in his voice when he said, "It's for you." But she had the tray ready with the whiskey and the ice cubes and the jigger and all when he got home at night, and that he liked. As for the children, at first they didn't want to have anything to do with her. The mistress explained that they were very attached to the previous mother's helper—a German girl who had left to get married —and she was not to mind. She didn't. That is, she didn't mind anything but the fact they were being brought up as heathens. So she told them about how the Jews crucified Our Lord, and about the Blessed Saints, and Mary and Joseph, and promised to take them to Mass, and in no time they were eating out of her hand.

She found out there were more bars and dance halls than you could shake a stick at, and she was in one or another of them five nights out of seven. The other two nights she went straight to bed as soon as she had pressed the button on the dishwashing machine. In a hamburger bar she met a boy with blond wavy hair who was an orphan like her, only he had been raised in a Home. Though he didn't say he was in love with her, still and all she liked him. He was interesting to talk to, because so many things seemed to have happened to him, and he didn't ask her to go home with him, so she had no chance to refuse. She didn't really expect to hear from him again, but he called the very next night. She met him in front of the movie house, and during the movie she could feel his arm resting lightly on the back of her seat, and once or twice he gave her shoulder a squeeze, but she didn't have to move her leg away or say "Don't." Afterward, they went to a bar on First Avenue. She told him all about her cousin's family in Glasgow, and about coming over on the boat, and the things she liked about Cathleen and the things she didn't like, and about the way it used to be at home before her mother died and she went to live with her grandmother. Finally she was all talked out, and she just sat there, feeling happy and peaceful. He said, "Another beer?" and she said no, and he had one last one, which he didn't spend any time over, and then he put his hand on the back of her neck and said, "Come on, baby, I'll walk you to your domicile." And that was what she thought they were doing, only when she looked up they were standing in front of the building where *he* lived. He said, "I just want to get a coat, I'm chilly," and she said, "I'll wait here," and he said, "At this time of night, in this neighborhood? Are you out of your mind?" So she followed him up six flights of stairs, and the first thing she knew she was having her clothes torn off her, and the rest she didn't remember. It was daylight when she got home, and she had to wake the night elevator man, who was married and cranky, and he made a fresh remark, which she ignored.

SHE went to church but she was afraid to go to confession, for fear the priest would find out she was an orphan and put her in a Home. If she had only saved her money, she could have got on the boat and gone back to Scotland, but she had bought clothes instead. Lots of clothes. The children's closets were full of them. She could hear her grandmother's voice saying, "You're going to the dogs," and it was true, she was. She also had a stomach ache, and it didn't go away. For three days she went around doubled up with the pain, and then the mistress noticed it and made her go to a doctor. They paid her wages while she was in the hospital having her appendix out, and for two weeks afterward, but they didn't want her to come back, because they had this colored woman, so she went to see the lady at the employment agency who had been so nice to her, only this time she was busy and somebody else gave her an address on Lexington Avenue, and on the way there she passed a bar-and-grill she liked the looks of. It was called Home on the Range, and it was pitch dark even in the daytime. Maybe I ought to start a New Life, the girl thought, and it turned out they did need a waitress, so that was that. Except that she wasn't forgotten. The children remembered her. Of all the maids, they liked her the best, and never forgot what she told them. And one night about a year after she left, the master was awakened out of a sound sleep by the ringing of the telephone, and a sad-voiced young man asked to speak to her. "No, you can't speak to her!" the master said indignantly. "Do you realize what time it is?" The sad voice seemed surprised to learn that it was the middle of the night, and unable to understand why anybody should mind being called at that hour, and unwilling to believe that the girl wasn't there.

5

The country where nobody ever grew old and died

THERE used to be, until roughly a hundred and fifty years ago, a country where nobody ever grew old and died. The gravestone with its weathered inscription, the wreath on the door, the black arm band, and the friendly reassuring smile of the undertaker were unknown there. This is not as strange as it at first seems. You do not have to look very far to find a woman who does not show her age or a man who intends to live forever. In this country, people did live forever, and nobody thought anything about it, but at some time or other somebody had thought about it, because there were certain restrictions on the freedom of the inhabitants. The country was not large, and there would soon not have been enough land to go around. So, instead of choosing an agreeable site and building a house on it, married couples chose an agreeable house and bought the right to add a story onto it. In this way, gradually, the houses, which were of stone, and square, and without superfluous ornamentation, became towers. The prevailing style of architecture was very much like that of the Italian hill towns. Arriving at the place where you lived, you rang the concierge's bell and sat down in a wicker swing, with your parcels on your lap, and were lifted to your own floor by ropes and pulleys.

A country where there were no children would be sadness incarnate. People didn't stop having them, but they were placed in such a way that the smallest number of children could be enjoyed by the greatest number of adults. If you wanted to raise a family, you applied for a permit and waited your turn. Very often by the time the permit came, the woman was too old to have a child and received instead a permit to help bring up somebody else's child.

Young women who were a pleasure to look at were enjoyed the way flowers are enjoyed, but leaving one's youth behind was not considered to be a catastrophe, and the attitudes and opinions of the young were not anxiously subscribed to. There is, in fact, some question whether the young of that country really were young, as we understand the word. Most people appeared to be on the borderline between maturity and early middle age, as in England in the late eighteenth century, when the bald pate and the head of thick brown hair were both concealed by a powdered wig, and physical deterioration was minimized by the fashions in dress and by what constituted good manners.

All the arts flourished except history. If you wanted to know what things were like in the period of Erasmus or Joan of Arc or Ethelred the Unready, you asked somebody who was alive at the time. People tended to wear the clothes of the period in which they came of age, and so walking down the street was like thumbing through a book on the history of costume. The soldiers, in every conceivable kind of armor and uniform, were a little boy's dream.

As one would expect, that indefatigable traveler Lady
Mary Wortley Montagu spent a considerable time in this
interesting country before she settled down in Venice, and
so did William Beckford. Lady Mary's letters about it were
destroyed by her daughter after her death, because they
happened to contain assertions of a shocking nature, for
which proof was lacking, about a contemporary figure
who would have relished a prosecution for libel. For Beckford's experiences, see his "Dreams, Waking Thoughts, and
Incidents" (Leipzig, 1832).

One might have supposed that in a country where death
was out of the question, morbidity would be unknown.
This was true for I have no idea how many centuries and
then something very strange happened. The young, until
this moment entirely docile and unimaginative, began having scandalous parties at which they pretended that they
were holding a funeral. They even went so far as to put
together a makeshift pine coffin, and took turns lying in it,
with their eyes closed and their hands crossed, and a lighted
candle at the head and foot. This occurred during Beckford's stay, and it is just possible that he had something to
do with it. Though he could be very amusing, he was a
natural mischief-maker and an extremely morbid man.

The mock funerals were the first thing that happened.
The second was the trial, *in absentia*, of a gypsy woman
who was accused of taking money with intent to defraud.
This was not an instance of a poor foolish widow's being
persuaded to bring her husband's savings to a fortuneteller
in order to have the money doubled. In the first place,
there were no widows, and the victim was a young man.

The plaintiff—just turned twenty-one, Beckford says,
and exceedingly handsome—stated under oath that he had
consulted the gypsy woman in the hope of learning from

her the secret of how to commit suicide. For it seems that in this country as everywhere else gypsies were a race apart and a law unto themselves. They did not choose to live forever, so they didn't. When one of them decided that life had no further interest for him, he did something. What, nobody knew. It was assumed that the gypsy bent on terminating his existence sat down under a tree or by a riverbank, some nice quiet place where he wouldn't be disturbed, and in a little while the other gypsies came and disposed of the body.

The plaintiff testified that the gypsy woman studied his hand, and then she looked in her crystal ball, and then she excused herself in order to get something on the other side of a curtain. That was the last anybody had seen of her or of the satchel full of money which the plaintiff had brought with him.

The idea that a personable young man, on the very threshold of life, had actually wanted to die caused a tremendous stir. The public was barred from the trial, but Beckford was on excellent terms with the wife of the Lord Chief Justice and managed to attend the hearing in the guise of a court stenographer. The story is to be found in the Leipzig edition of his book and no other, which suggests that he perhaps did have something to do with the events he describes, and that from feelings of remorse, or shame, wrote about them and then afterwards wished to suppress what he had written. At all events we have his very interesting account. The jury found for the plaintiff and against the gypsy woman. After the verdict was read aloud in the court, the attorney for the defense made an impassioned and—in the light of what happened afterward —heartbreaking speech. If only it had been taken seriously! He asked that the verdict stand, but that no effort be made to find his client, and that no other gypsy be questioned or molested in any way by the police. The court saw the matter in a different light, and during the next few days the police set about rounding up every single gypsy in the country. The particular gypsy woman who had victimized the young man with a bent for self-destruction was never found. The others were subjected to the most detailed questioning. When that produced no information, the rack and the thumbscrew were applied, to no purpose. You might as well try to squeeze kindness out of a stone as torture a secret out of a gypsy. But there was living with the gypsies at that time a middle-aged man who had been stolen by them as a child and who had spent his life among them. When he was brought into the courtroom between two bailiffs, the attorney for the defense lowered his head and covered his eyes with his hand. The man was put on the witness stand and, pale and drawn after a night of torture, gave his testimony. Shortly after this, the gravestone, the wreath, the arm band, and the smiling undertaker, so familiar everywhere else in the world, made their appearance here also, and the country was no longer unique.

6

The woman who lived beside

a running stream

THERE was an old woman whose house was beside a
bend in a running stream. Sometimes the eddying current sounded almost like words, like a message: *Rill, you
will, you will, sill, rillable, syllable, billable.* . . . Sometimes
when she woke in the night it was to the sound of a fountain plashing, though there wasn't, of course, any fountain.
Or sometimes it sounded like rain, though the sky was clear
and full of stars.

Around her cottage Canada lilies grew, and wild pepper-
mint, and lupins, Queen Anne's lace taller than her head,
and wild roses that were half the ordinary size, and the
wind brought with it across somebody else's pasture the
smell of pine trees, which she could see from her kitchen
window. Here she lived, all by herself, and since she had no
one to cook and care for but herself, you might think that
time was heavy on her hands. It was just the contrary. The
light woke her in the morning, and the first thing she heard
was the sound of the running stream. It was the sound of
hurry, and she said to herself, "I must get up and get breakfast and make the bed and sweep, or I'll be late setting the

bread to rise." And when the bread was out of the way, there was the laundry. And when the laundry was hanging on the line, there was something else that urgently needed doing. The stream also never stopped hurrying and worrying on to some place she had never thought about and did not try to imagine. So great was its eagerness that it cut away at its banks until every so often it broke through to some bend farther on, leaving a winding bog that soon filled up with wild flowers. But this the old woman had no way of knowing, for when she left the house it was to buy groceries in the store at the crossroads, or call on a sick friend. She was not much of a walker. She suffered from shortness of breath, and her knees bothered her a good deal. "The truth is," she kept telling herself, as if it was an idea she had not yet completely accepted, "I am an old woman, and I don't have forever to do the things that need to be done." Looking in the mirror, she could not help seeing the wrinkles. And her hair, which had once been thick and shining, was not only gray but so thin she could see her scalp. Even the texture of her hair had changed. It was frizzy, and the hair of a stranger. "So long ago," she said to herself as she read through old letters before destroying them. "And it seems like yesterday." And as she wrote out labels, which she pasted on the undersides of tables and chairs, telling whom they were to go to after her death, she said, "I don't see how I could have accumulated so much. Where did it all come from?" And one morning she woke up with the realization that if she died that day, she would have done all she could do. Her dresser drawers were tidied, the cupboards in order. It was a Tuesday, and she did not bake until Thursday, and the marketing she had done the day before. The house was clean, the ironing put away, and if she threw the covers off and hurried into her clothes, it would be to do something that didn't really need doing. So she lay there thinking, and gradually the thoughts in her mind, which were threadbare with repetition, were replaced by the sound of conversation that came to her from outside— *rill, you will? You will, still. But fill, but fill*—and the chittering conversation of the birds. Suddenly she knew what she was going to do, though there was no hurry about it. She was going to follow the stream and see what happened to it after it passed her house.

She ate a leisurely breakfast, washed the dishes, and put a sugar sandwich and an orange in a brown paper bag. Then, wearing a black straw hat in case it should turn warm and an old gray sweater in case it should turn cold, she locked the house up, and put the key to the front door under the mat, and started off.

THE first thing she came to was a rustic foot-bridge, which seemed to lead to an island, but the island turned out to be merely the other side of the stream. Here there were paths everywhere, made by the horses in the pasture coming down to drink. She followed now one, now another, stepping over fallen tree trunks, and pausing when her dress caught on a briar. Sometimes the path led her to the brink of the stream at a place where there was no way to cross, and she had to retrace her steps and choose some other path. Sometimes it led her through a cool glade, or a meadow where the grass grew up to her knees. When she came to a barbed-wire fence with a stile over it, she knew she was following a path made by human beings.

First she was on one side of the stream and then, when a big log or a bridge invited her to cross over, she was on the other. She saw a house, but it was closed and shuttered, and so, though she knew she was trespassing, she felt no alarm. When the path left the stream, she decided to continue on it, assuming that the stream would quickly wind back upon itself and rejoin her. The path led her to a road, and the road led her to a gate with a sign on it: "KEEP THIS GATE CLOSED." It was standing open. She went on, following the road as before, and came to another gate, with a padlock and chain on it, but right beside the gate was an opening in the fence just large enough for her to crawl through. The road was deep in dust and lined with tall trees that cast a dense shade. She saw a deer, which stopped grazing and raised its head to look at her, and then went bounding off. The road brought her to more houses —summer cottages, not places where people lived the year round. To avoid them she cut through the trees, in the direction that she assumed the running stream must be, and saw still another house. Here, for the first time, there was somebody—a man who did not immediately see her, for he was bent over, sharpening a scythe.

"I'm looking for the little running stream," she said to him.

"You left that a long way back," the man said. "The river is just on the other side of those big pine trees."

"Is there a bridge?"

"Half a mile upstream."

"What happens if I follow the river downstream on this side?"

"You can't," the man said. "There's no way. You have to go upstream to the bridge."

Should she turn around and go home, she wondered. The sun was not yet overhead, so she walked on, toward the trees the man had pointed to, thinking that he might be mistaken and that it might be the running stream that went past her house, but it wasn't. It was three times as broad, and clearly a little river. It too was lined with wild flowers, and in places they had leaped over the flowing water and were growing out of a log in midstream. The river was almost as clear as the air, and she could see the bottom, and schools of fish darting this way and that. Rainbow trout, they were. Half a mile upstream and half a mile down made a mile, and she thought of her poor knees. The water, though swift, was apparently quite shallow. She could take off her shoes and stockings and wade across.

Holding her skirts up, she went slowly out into the river. The bottom was all smooth, rounded stones, precarious to walk on, and she was careful to place her feet firmly. When she was halfway across she stepped into a deep hole, lost her balance, and fell. She tried to stand up, but the current was too swift, and she was hampered by her wet clothing. Gasping and swallowing water, she was tumbled over and over as things are that float downstream in a rushing current. "I did not think my life would end like this," she said to herself, and gave up and let the current take her.

When she opened her eyes, she was lying on the farther bank of the river. She must have been lying there for hours, because her hair and her clothing were dry. In the middle of the river there was a young man, who turned his head and smiled at her. He had blond hair and he was not more than twenty, and he had waders on which came up to his waist, and his chest and shoulders were bare, and she could see right through him; she could see the river and the wild flowers on the other bank. Had he pulled her out? You can't see through living people. He must be dead. But he was not a corpse, he was the most angelic young man she had ever seen, and radiantly happy as he whipped his line back and forth over the shining water.

And so, for that matter, was she. She tried to speak to him but could not. It was too strange.

He waded downstream slowly, casting as he went, and she watched him until he was out of sight. She saw that there was a path that followed the river downstream. I'll just go a little farther, she thought, and started on. She wanted to have another look at the beautiful young man, who must be just around the next bend of the river. Instead, when she got there, she saw a heavy, middle-aged man with a bald head. He also was standing in the middle of the river, casting, and a shaft of sunlight passed right through him. She went on. The path was only a few feet from the water, and it curved around the roots of old trees to avoid a clump of bushes. She saw two horses standing by the mouth of a little stream that might be the stream that went past her house—there was no way of telling—and she could see right through them, too, as if they were made of glass. Soon after this she began to overtake people on the path—for her knees no longer bothered her, and she walked quite fast, for the pleasure of it, and because she had such a feeling of lightness. She saw, sitting on the bank, a boy with a great many freckles, who caught a good-sized trout while she stood watching him. He smiled at her and she smiled back at him, and went on. She met a very friendly dog, who stayed with her, and a young woman with a baby carriage, and an old man. They both smiled at her, the way the young man and the boy had, but said nothing. The feeling of lightness persisted, as if a burden larger than she had realized had been taken off her shoulders. If I keep on much farther, I'll never find my way home, she thought. But nevertheless she went on, as if she had no choice, meeting more people, and suddenly she looked down at her hands and saw that they too were

transparent. Then she knew. But without any fear or regret. So it was there all the time, an hour's walk from the
house, she thought. And with a light heart she walked on,
enjoying the day and the sunlight on the river, which
seemed almost alive, and from time to time meeting more
people all going the same way she was, all going the same
way as the river.

7

The marble watch

O NCE upon a time there was a country so large that messengers journeying from the capital to the frontier were often never heard from again. The royal palace was immense, the palace grounds occupied thousands of acres, and rescue parties had to be sent out to locate important personages who had got confused and lost their way in the rose garden. The King's guard was made up entirely of men who were seven feet tall, and the horses that drew his enormous gilded coach were as broad as Percherons. And the courtiers often had trouble staying awake during the King's witty remarks, which, like his gestures, were modelled on those of his royal father, known in history books as Charles the Ponderous. At court concerts, the program listed various symphonies, concertos, *divertimenti* for strings and oboe, quartets, quintets, and what have you, but the musicians played only the largo and lento movements, omitting both the allegro vivace at the beginning and the presto at the end, in the belief that they were impossible to play and would no doubt be nerve-racking to have to hear. At the court balls, there was an interval of an hour or so between minuets, during which the dancers fanned themselves and recovered their breath. A simple audience with the King went on all day, without accomplishing anything. The royal proclamations, read in every square and market place in the kingdom, took up so much time and were so packed with polysyllabic words of Latin derivation that when the inhabitants were free to return to their plows and shoemaker's benches, their looms and churns and shops, they found that their minds were slow and listless, and very little work was done in this once prosperous kingdom. The imports exceeded the exports by several milliards of pounds sterling, and the currency was so inflated that arithmetic was no longer useful in settling accounts and bookkeepers had to resort to differential calculus and a slide rule.

It took the King a long time to realize that something was wrong and another five years to consider carefully what he ought to do about it. The council of state had not met since his father's time, and when it finally convened, at his order, the King's opening remarks took three weeks, after which the council adjourned and met again in the following autumn. The chancellor of the exchequer estimated expenditures for the next nine years at rather more than thirty times expenditures for the past nine years, and revenues at one one-hundredth of expenditures. The evening papers reported that in general the chancellor's tone was optimistic and appeared to satisfy the King and council. During the next three days the members of the council rose, one after another, and begged for a further adjournment, on the ground that they needed time and statisticians to consider the difficulty that had been placed before them. The only dissenting voice was that of the royal astronomer, who, with long, long pauses after each word, said, "My lord, the stars are moving much more quickly than they used to, or else we are moving more slowly, and it is my opinion that the root of the trouble lies—"

"Louder!" called a voice at the back of the council chamber, which held five thousand people. "We can't hear you back here."

"No one knows exactly what day of the week it is," the astronomer said. "And speaking for myself, I cannot say that I am even sure of the month. Every year the earth grows more out of touch with the sky."

"In your royal father's time," the astronomer continued, when the council convened the next morning, "many people had watches and could tell the time of day, and the clever ones were able to keep track of what day of the week it was, and even to predict more or less accurately the end of one month and the beginning of another. It is my opinion that we should, with Your Majesty's approval and encouragement, construct a timepiece."

"But if there were so many watches in our father's reign, why construct one?" said the King. "There must still be a timepiece somewhere."

"Your Majesty," said the astronomer, "I have inquired exhaustively into the matter, and while it is true that here and there, in remote districts, it is still possible to locate a timepiece, they have not been wound for decades, the works are corroded with rust, and they do not keep time at all, let alone the precise mathematical time that would serve our present purposes. What we need, in my humble opinion, is a watch that can be wound and will run."

"We seem to remember a watch heavily encrusted with jewels that was presented to us by a visiting potentate," said the King, "on our tenth birthday. But it was all so long ago. No doubt that watch has been mislaid."

The chancellor of the exchequer rose and stated categorically that the watch in question had not been mislaid. "I cannot put my hand on it at a moment's notice," he said, "but I know I saw it listed in a survey of the royal assets, five or ten years ago."

"If it was listed in the survey," the King said, "then it must be somewhere. In the sub-basement of the treasury, perhaps. But I dare say that, like the others, it has grown rusty. But tell me," he said, turning back to the astronomer, "were not the watches that people carried during the reign of our father very small—so small they could be carried in a man's vest pocket? And were not the works flimsy? And did not those watches have to be wound once a day?"

"Even so, Your Majesty. The cases were sometimes of silver and gold, but the works that hurried the hour and the minute hand round and round and in this way indicated the rushing of time were exceedingly delicate, and the watches had to be wound once a day, preferably at bedtime."

"That's what we thought," said the King. "And if you dropped one of these watches, did it not break, and have to be left at the watch-mender's for weeks at a time while it was being repaired, with the result that the person or persons who carried it had no way of telling the time?"

"There was that difficulty," the astronomer admitted. "And would be again, unless we constructed an alternate watch, to be referred to on those occasions when—"

"It seems hardly fitting that a kingdom the size of this be run according to an instrument so undependable and so unimpressive," said the King. "If you are truly convinced that a watch will bring the earth closer to the sky and, incidentally, improve the condition of the treasury, then we will construct a watch and see that all civil, ecclesiastical, and court activities conform to it. But we will construct this timepiece of some appropriate material. Something solid, durable, and rustproof, that will not need tinkering with or constant winding. Let the watch be constructed of marble."

THE construction of a marble watch, the first ever attempted, so far as anybody knows, went on without interruption, diligently, for fifteen years, during which time the inhabitants of the kingdom grew threadbare, and the treasury used up its last resources on the quarrying and cutting of snow-white stone. The court astronomer had a nervous breakdown and was replaced by his assistant, who in turn died of a broken heart. The work was carried on by one person and another up until the very day the kingdom was invaded by an army from one of the very small but active neighboring kingdoms. The enemy troops were in possession of the capital before the people realized that their country had been invaded. The King escaped with his life and the blueprints of the great Timepiece.

He hid first in the hut of a fisherman on the shore of a lake so broad that even on a clear day you could not see the opposite shore. Then he was sheltered by a charcoal burner whose hut was in the shadow of a mountain so tall that the snow-covered peak was usually hidden by clouds. And finally he was driven to accept the hospitality of a poor poacher who lived by snaring rabbits in a wood so dense that no man had ever penetrated more than halfway through it. In the course of these successive flights, the King lost weight, learned to move quickly, to eat and sleep in snatches, and to speak sometimes with admirable conciseness, on the run. Since there was no court, there were no court proclamations that needed composing. The poacher's wife and daughter were busy with their own affairs, which were never affairs of state, and so he could not offer his opinion about the way they were conducted. The occasional messengers and spies brought only discouraging news, and the King devoted himself to the study of natural history. Many of the birds and beasts that he watched were, he could not help noticing, extremely small, and some of the insects were so minute that they might easily have served as parts of the old-fashioned watches that people carried during the reign of his father. Even so, it appeared that by their smallness and quickness they were often able to escape from or defend themselves against their natural enemies. The ants particularly commanded the King's respect and attention. After observing them for some time, he settled the question of the royal succession by marrying the poacher's quite charming daughter, and thereby rid himself of the only one of his problems that was at all pressing.

After a short interval, a mere nine or ten months, she presented him with a son, and during the baptism of the Heir Apparent at a forest spring a messenger arrived with mud on his boots and his horse in a lather. The enemy—never, it seemed, very large in number—had grown weary of subjugating so inactive a country, had provoked a war with another small neighboring state, and had not been heard of for nearly six months. It was presumed that either they had been defeated in battle and perhaps perished or else they had simply got lost somewhere between the capital and the frontier and were wandering around, helpless and incapable of further harm. At all events, there was no longer any reason why the King should not return and rule over his people. Unfortunately, the messenger added, the enemy's last outrageous act before they departed on their warlike expedition had been to pull down the royal palace, but the Royal College of Architects was already at work on the design for a new palace that would far surpass, in size and splendor, the one that had been destroyed.

The King and Queen and Heir Apparent travelled all the way through crowds that were half naked but not listless, and that indeed often cheered quite energetically. The King pitched a tent in the rose garden, now overgrown with brambles, and sent for the College of Architects. Together they went through the plans for the new palace, while the Queen looked over the King's shoulder.

"Much too extensive," he said, astonishing everyone by the quickness of his decision and the brevity with which it was conveyed. "By your own least conservative estimate, the quarrying and cutting of that much marble will take fifty years. Possibly longer. I am not a young man and this tent leaks. Since it is traditional that the king live in a marble palace, I must, I suppose, follow the custom of my ancestors, though wood, I have recently discovered, is easier to heat and less clammy on damp days— Did the enemy carry watches?"

"No, Your Majesty," said the Architect Royal. "They were so quick in everything they did that they seemed not to know or care what time it was."

"The great Timepiece was not destroyed along with the palace?"

The Architect Royal shook his head. "There was talk of destroying it, but the enemy general paid a visit to the site of this magnificent experiment and was so impressed that he said, 'Let it be. If we destroy it, nobody will ever believe that people are as foolish as they really are.' "

"I see," said the King, and for several minutes he remained deep in thought. At last he roused himself and said, "Fine. There ought to be just enough marble in that uncompleted watch to construct a palace the size of the poacher's hut, for which Her Majesty is, quite naturally, homesick. A week ought to be ample time for drawing up the plans and executing them. And if you can locate an ant's nest, will you transport that also to the palace courtyard, and then go on about your business."

A LL this, being the King's decree, was done, and in no time at all the want of equilibrium between exports and imports was a thing of the past. At court concerts, musical compositions were played straight through from beginning to end. At court balls, the minuet gave way to the waltz and the mazurka. The Queen got over her homesickness, and the King, observing the ant colony whenever he had some decision of great moment to make, soon brought on an era of such prosperity that he is referred to in all the history books as "Charles the Expediter" and by the common people, affectionately, as "Charles the Flea."

8

The half-crazy woman

ONCE upon a time there was a half-crazy woman who lived off the leavings of other people, who shook their heads when they saw her coming, and tried not to get in conversation with her. They wanted to be kind, but there is a limit to kindness, and the half-crazy woman was so distracted that anyone listening to her began to feel half crazy too. Since people avoided her, she talked to any stray dog or cat that came along, and sometimes even to the old willow tree that grew by her door. One autumn evening when the weight around her heart was too heavy to bear, she went outside to the sty where she kept her thin, disgruntled pig and said sorrowfully, "Pig, you won't die of hunger, will you?"

The pig said, "No, I won't die of hunger."

"Thank you for that," the half-crazy woman said, but she was not satisfied. The pig had had nothing to eat for three days.

She went back into the house and saw the fire burning low on the hearth and said, "Fire, you won't go out, will you?"

The fire said, "No, I won't go out."

"Thank you for that," the half-crazy woman said, and tried not to worry, even though there was only an armful of faggots to last all night.

But then she remembered the bread baking in the oven. She opened the oven door and looked in and saw the loaf baking from the heat of the stones in the chimney and thought, What if I should forget to take it out? What if the loaf should burn?

She said anxiously, "Loaf, you won't burn, will you?"

The loaf said, "No, I won't burn."

"Thank you for that," the half-crazy woman said, and thought, Now I have nothing to trouble me.

But the wind, rising, shook the walls and rattled the door of her poor cottage, and so she lit a candle and went up the ladder that led to the attic. The attic was low and she could barely stand upright. She heard the wind straining at the eaves and thought how old the house was, and how poorly built, and she put her hand up and said, "Roof over my head, you won't blow away, will you?"

The roof said, "No, I won't blow away."

"Thank you for that," the half-crazy woman said, and tried to feel happy, but happiness doesn't come for the asking, and there was a musty smell in the attic that she couldn't account for. It was not the smell of old clothes, or of dust, or of leather, exactly, but something of all of these things, and it added to the weight around her heart. It must be the smell of Death, she thought, and in that very instant felt his presence there, in her empty attic. He was standing behind her, close enough to make the hairs on the back of her neck stiffen and rise. "Death, you won't ever leave me, will you?" she cried, and was frightened at the sound of her own words.

"No, I won't ever leave you," Death said. "You don't

have to worry. Go downstairs and take the loaf out of the oven before it burns and throw some wood on the fire before it goes out and feed the pig before it dies of hunger."

"Thank you for that," the half-crazy woman said, and climbed down the ladder and took the loaf, which was a golden brown, out of the oven, and threw some faggots on the fire, which blazed up brightly, and took some scraps that she had been saving for her own supper out to the pig. The wind had died down suddenly, and the half-crazy woman saw that it was going to be a calm clear night with millions of stars in the heavens. She found a stick and scratched the pig's back until it grunted with pleasure. Then she went into the house and cut a slice from the warm loaf and ate it by the fire. The weight was gone from around her heart. She thought of the presence waiting in the attic and listened but there was no sound. The house was still. And the half-crazy woman knew for the first time what it is to have peace of mind.

9

The two women friends

THERE were two women, well along in years, and one lived in a castle and one lived in the largest house in the village that was at the foot of the castle rock. Though picturesque, the castle had bathrooms and central heating, and it would not for very long have withstood a siege, no matter how antiquated the weapons employed. The village was also picturesque, being made up of a single street of thatched Elizabethan cottages. The two women were friends, and if one had weekend guests it was understood that the other would stand by, ready to entertain them. When the conversation threatened to run out, guests at Cleeve Castle were taken to Cleeve House and offered tea and hot buttered scones, under a canopy of apple blossoms or in front of a roaring fire, according to the season. The largest house in the village had been made by joining three of the oldest cottages together, and the catalogue of its inconveniences often made visitors wipe tears of amusement from their eyes. The inconveniences were mostly felt by the servants, who had to carry cans of hot water and breakfast trays up the treacherous stairs, and who, when they were in a hurry, tripped over the uneven

doorsills and bumped their heads on low beams. Guests at
Cleeve House were taken to the castle and plied with gin
and ghost stories.

One would have expected this arrangement, so useful to
both women, to be lasting, but the friendship of women
seems always to have embedded in it somewhere a fishhook,
and as it happened the mistress of Cleeve House was born
with a heavier silver spoon in her mouth, and baptized in a
longer christening gown, and in numerous other ways was
socially more enviable. On the other hand, the money that
had originally gone with the social advantages was, alas,
rather run out, and it was without the slightest trace of
anxiety that the woman in the castle sat down to balance
her checkbook. Weekend guests at the castle tended to be
more important politically or in the world of the arts—
flashy, in short. And the weekend guests at Cleeve House
more important to know if it was a question of getting
your children into the right schools or yourself into the
right clubs. In a word, nobby. But how the woman who
lived in the castle could have dreamed for one minute that
she could entertain a member of the royal family and not
bring him to tea at Cleeve House, to be amused by the
catalogue of its inconveniences and the story of how it
came to be thrown together out of three dark, cramped
little cottages by an architect who was a disciple of William
Morris, it is hard to say. Perhaps the friendship had begun
to seem burdensome and the duties one-sided. Or perhaps it
was the gradual accumulation of tactful silences, which
avoided saying that the woman who lived in the village was
top drawer and the woman who lived in the castle was not,
and careless remarks, such as anybody might be guilty of
with a close friend, which frankly admitted it. In any
event, one does not go running here, there, and everywhere

with a member of the royal family in tow. There is pro-
tocol to be observed, secretaries and chauffeurs and valets
have to be consulted, and the conversation doesn't threaten
to run out because what you have, in these circumstances,
isn't conversation in the usual sense of the word. But anyway, the mistress of Cleeve House sat waiting for the telephone to ring, with the wrinkles ironed out of her best
tablecloth, and her Spode tea set brought down from the
highest shelf of the china closet, and the teaspoons polished
till you could see your face in them, and her Fortuny gown
taken out of its plastic bag and left to hang from the bedroom chandelier. And, unbelievably, the telephone did not
ring. In the middle of the afternoon she had the operator
check her phone to see if it was out of order. This was a
mistake, because in a village people are very apt to put two
and two together. By nightfall it was known all up and
down the High Street that her in the castle was entertaining royalty and had left her in the big house to sit and
twiddle her thumbs.

Not that the mistress of Cleeve House cared one way or
the other about the royal family. No, it was merely the
slight to a friendship of very long standing that disturbed
her. And for the sake of that friendship, though it cost her
a struggle, she was prepared to act as if nothing unusual
had happened when the telephone rang on Sunday morning, and to suggest that the mistress of Cleeve Castle bring
her guests to tea. The telephone rang on Monday morning
instead. To anyone listening in, and several people were, it
was clear that she was speaking a little too much as if nothing unusual had happened. However, the invitation—to
drive, just the two of them, in the little car, over to the
market town and have lunch at the Star and Garter—was
accepted. And because one does not entertain royalty and

then not mention it, the subject came up finally, in the most
natural way, and the mistress of Cleeve House was able to
achieve the tone she wanted, which was a mixture of reasonable curiosity and amused indifference. But it was all
over between them, and they both knew it.

They continued to see each other, less often and less
intimately, for another three or four months, and then the
woman who lived in the largest house in the village finished
it off in a way that made it possible for her to carry her
head high. The husband of the woman who lived in the
castle had, unwisely, allowed his name to be put up for a
London club that was rather too grand for a man who had
made a fortune in wholesale poultry. Even so, with a great
deal of help from various quarters or a little help from the
right quarter, he might have made it. There were two or
three men who could have pulled this off single-handed,
and when one of them came down to Cleeve House for the
weekend, it was the turn of the mistress of the castle to sit
and wait for the telephone to ring. On Monday morning,
the nanny of the children of Cleeve House (who were
really the woman's grandchildren) took them to play with
the children of the castle, as she had been doing every
Monday morning all summer, and was told at the castle
gate that the children of the castle were otherwise occupied. Though they had not been in any way involved and
did not even know the cause of the falling out, the children
of the castle and the children of Cleeve House were enemies from that day forth, and so were their nannies. The
two husbands, being more worldly, still exchanged curt
nods when they met in the High Street or on the railway
platform. As for the two women, they very cleverly managed never even to set eyes on one another.

Weekend guests at Cleeve House were taken for a walk,

naturally, because it was one of the oldest villages in England, and when they saw the castle, with rooks roosting in the apertures of the keep, they cried out with pleasure at finding a place so picturesque that near London. When the mistress of Cleeve House explained that she was no longer on friendly terms with the castle, their faces betrayed their disappointment. And with a consistency that was really extraordinary, people who were staying at Cleeve Castle sooner or later came back from a walk saying, "The village is charming, I must say. But who is that fascinating gray-haired woman who walks with a stick and lives in that largish house on the High Street? We're dying to meet her."

CITY people get over their anger, as a rule, but it is different if you live in a village. For one thing, everybody knows that you are angry, and why, and the slightest shift in position is publicly commented on, and this stiffens the antagonism and makes it permanent. Something very large indeed—a fire, or a flood, a war, a catastrophe of some sort—is required to bring about a reconciliation and push the injured parties into one another's outstretched arms.

One winter morning, the village learned, via the wireless, that it was in the direct path of a new eight-lane expressway connecting London and the seacoast. The money for it had been appropriated and it was too late to prevent the road from being built, but the political connections of Cleeve Castle working hand in glove with the social connections of Cleeve House could perhaps divert it so that some other village was obliterated. After deliberating for days, the woman who lived in the castle picked up the telephone and called Cleeve House, but while the telephone was still ringing she hung up. The injury to her husband (what a way to repay a thousand kindnesses!) was still too fresh in her mind. There must be some other way of dealing with the problem, she told herself, and sitting down at her desk she wrote a long and affectionate letter to a school friend who was married to a Member of Parliament, imploring his help.

After considering the situation from every angle, the woman who lived in the largest house in the village came to the only sensible conclusion, which was that some things are worth swallowing your pride for, and she put on her hat and coat and walked up to the castle. But when she came to the castle gate, the memory of how her grandchildren had been turned away (the smallness of it!) filled her with anger, and she paid a call on the vicar instead.

In due time the surveyors appeared, with their tripods, sighting instruments, chains, stakes, and red flags, and the path of doom was made clear. The government, moved by humane considerations, did, however, build a new village. The cottages of Upper Cleeve, as it was called, were all exactly alike and as ugly as sin. There was no way on earth that you could join three of them together and produce a house that William Morris would have felt at home in. The castle was saved by its rocky situation, but its owners did not choose to look out on an eight-lane expressway and breathe exhaust fumes and be kept awake all night long by trucks and trailers. So the rooks fell heir to it.

10

The fisherman who had no one to go out in his boat with him

O NCE upon a time there was a poor fisherman who
had no one to go out in his boat with him. The
man he started going out with when he was still a boy
was now crippled with rheumatism and sat all day by
the fire. The other fishermen were all paired off, and
there was nobody for him. Out on the water, without
a soul to talk to, the hours between daybreak and late afternoon were very long, and to pass the time he sang. He sang
the songs that other people sang, whatever he had heard,
and this was of course a good deal in the way of music, because in the olden times people sang more than they do
now. But eventually he came to the end of all the songs he
knew or had ever heard and wanted to learn some new
songs. He knew that they were written down and published, but this was no help to him because he had never
been to school and didn't know how to read words, let
alone the musical staff. You might as well have presented
him with a clay tablet of Egyptian hieroglyphics. But
there were ways, and he took advantage of them. At a cer-

tain time, on certain days of the week, the children in the schoolhouse had singing, and he managed to be in the vicinity. He brought his boat in earlier those days, on one pretext or another, and stood outside the school building. At first the teacher was mystified, but he saw that the poor fisherman always went away as soon as the singing lesson was over, and putting two and two together he realized why the man was there. So, one day, he went to the door and invited the fisherman in. The fisherman backed away, and then he turned and hurried off down the road to the beach. But the next time they had singing, there he was. The schoolteacher opened a window so the fisherman could hear better and went on with the lesson. While the children were singing "There were three sisters fair and bright," the door opened slowly. The teacher pointed to a desk in the back row, and the fisherman squeezed himself into it, though it was a child's desk and much too small for him. The children waved their hands in the air and asked silly questions and giggled, but, never having been to school, the fisherman thought this was customary and did not realize that he was creating a disturbance. He came again, and again.

People manage to believe in magic—of one kind or another. And ghosts. And the influence of the stars. And reincarnation. And a life everlasting. But not enough room is allowed for strangeness: that birds and animals know the way home; that a blind man, having sensed the presence of a wall, knows as well where to walk as you or I; that there have been many recorded instances of conversations between two persons who did not speak the same language but, each speaking his own, nevertheless understood each other perfectly. When the teacher passed out the songbooks, he gave one to the fisherman, well aware that his only contact with the printed page was through his huge, calloused hands. And time after time the fisherman knew, before the children opened their mouths and began to sing, what the first phrase would be, and where the song would go from there.

Naturally, he did not catch as many fish as he had when he was attending to his proper work, and sometimes there was nothing in the house to eat. His wife could not complain, because she was a deaf-mute. She was not ugly, but no one else would have her. Though she had never heard the sound of her own voice, or indeed any sound whatever, she could have made him feel her dissatisfaction, but she saw that what he was doing was important to him, and did not interfere. What the fisherman would have liked would have been to sing with the children when they sang, but his voice was so deep there was no possibility of its blending unnoticeably with theirs, so he sat in silence, and only when he was out in his boat did the songs burst forth from his throat. What with the wind and the sea birds' crying, he had to sing openly or he would not have known he was singing at all. If he had been on shore, in a quiet room, the sound would have seemed tremendous. Out under the sky, it merely seemed like a man singing.

He often thought that if there had only been a child in the house he could have sung the child to sleep, and that would have been pleasant. He would have sung to his wife if she could have heard him, and he did try, on his fingers, to convey the sound of music—the way the sounds fell together, the rising and descending, the sudden changes in tempo, and the pleasure of expecting to hear this note and hearing, instead, a different one, but she only smiled at him uncomprehendingly.

The schoolteacher knew that if it had been curiosity alone that drew the fisherman to the schoolhouse at the time of singing lessons, he would have stopped coming as soon as his curiosity was satisfied, and he didn't stop coming, which must mean that there was a possibility that he was innately musical. So he stopped the fisherman one day when they met by accident, and asked him to sing the scale. The fisherman opened his mouth and no sound came. He and the schoolteacher looked at each other, and then the fisherman colored, and hung his head. The schoolteacher clapped him on the shoulder and walked on, satisfied that what there was here was the love of music rather than a talent for it, and even that seemed to him something hardly short of a miracle.

IN those islands, storms were not uncommon and they were full of peril. Even large sailing ships were washed on the rocks and broken to pieces. As for the little boats the fishermen went out in, one moment they would be bobbing on the waves like a cork, now on the crest and now out of sight in a trough, and then suddenly there wasn't any boat. The sea would have swallowed it, and the men in it, in the blinking of an eye. It was a terrible fact that the islanders had learned to live with. If they had not been fishermen, they would have starved, so they continued to go out in their boats, and to read the sky for warnings, which were usually dependable, but every now and then a storm—and usually the very worst kind—would come up without any warning, or with only a short time between the first alarming change in the odor of the air, the first wisps of storm clouds, and the sudden lashing of the waters. When this happened, the women gathered on the shore and prayed. Sometimes they waited all night, and sometimes they waited in vain.

One evening, the fisherman didn't come home at the

usual time. His wife could not hear the wind or the shutters banging, but when the wind blew puffs of smoke down the chimney, she knew that a storm had come up. She put on her cloak, and wrapped a heavy scarf around her head, and started for the strand, to see if the boats were drawn up there. Instead, she found the other women waiting with their faces all stamped with the same frightened look. Usually the sea birds circled above the beach, waiting for the fishing boats to come in and the fishermen to cut open their fish and throw them the guts, but this evening there were no gulls or cormorants. The air was empty. The wind had blown them all inland, just as, by a freak, it had blown the boats all together, out on the water, so close that it took great skill to keep them from knocking against each other and capsizing in the dark. The fishermen called back and forth for a time, and then they fell silent. The wind had grown higher and higher, and the words were blown right out of their mouths, and they could not even hear themselves what they were saying. The wind was so high and the sound so loud that it was like a silence, and out of this silence, suddenly, came the sound of singing. Being poor ignorant fishermen, they did the first thing that occurred to them—they fell on their knees and prayed. The singing went on and on, in a voice that none of them had ever heard, and so powerful and rich and deep it seemed to come from the same place that the storm came from. A flash of lightning revealed that it was not an angel, as they thought, but the fisherman who was married to the deaf-mute. He was standing in his boat, with his head bared, singing, and in their minds this was no stranger or less miraculous than an angel would have been. They crossed themselves and went on praying, and the fisherman went on singing, and in a little while the waves began to grow smaller and the wind to abate, and the storm, which should have taken days to blow itself out, suddenly turned into an intense calm. As suddenly as it had begun, the singing stopped. The boats drew apart as in one boat after another the men took up their oars again, and in a silvery brightness, all in a cluster, the fishing fleet came safely in to shore.

II

The carpenter

ONCE upon a time there was a man of no particular age, a carpenter, whom all kinds of people entrusted with their secrets. Perhaps the smell of glue and sawdust and fresh-cut boards had something to do with it, but in any case he was not a troublemaker, and a secret is nearly always something that, if it became known, would make trouble for somebody. So they came to his shop, closed the door softly behind them, sat down on a pile of lumber, and pretended that they had come because they enjoyed watching him work. Actually, they did enjoy it. Some of them. His big square hands knew what they were doing, and all his movements were relaxed and skillful. The shavings curled up out of his plane as if the idea was to make long, beautiful shavings. He used his carpenter's rule and stubby pencil as if he were applying a moral principle. When he sawed, it seemed to have the even rhythm of his heartbeat. Though the caller might forget for five minutes what brought him here, in the end he stopped being interested in carpentry and said, "I know I can trust you, because you never repeat anything . . ." and there it was, one more secret added to the collection, a piece of information that, if it had got out, would have broken up a friendship or caused a son to be disinherited or ruined a half-happy marriage or cost some man his job or made trouble for somebody.

The carpenter had discovered that the best way to deal with this information that must not be repeated was to forget it as quickly as possible, though sometimes the secret was so strange he could not forget it immediately, and that evening his wife would ask, "Who was in the shop today?" For people with no children have only each other to spy on, and he was an open book to her.

Sometimes the person who had confided in him seemed afterward to have no recollection of having done this, and more than once the carpenter found himself wondering if he had imagined or misremembered something that he knew perfectly well he had not imagined and would remember to his dying day. In the middle of the night, if he had a wakeful period, instead of thrashing around in the bed and disturbing his wife's sleep, he lay quietly with his eyes open in the dark and was a spectator to plays in which honorable men were obliged to tell lies, the kind and good were a prey to lechery, the old acted not merely without wisdom but without common sense, debts were repaid not in kind but in hatred, and the young rode roughshod over everybody. When he had had enough of human nature, he put all these puppets back in their box and fell into a dreamless sleep.

For many years his life was like this, but it is a mistake to assume that people never change. They don't and they do change. Without his being able to say just when it happened and whether the change was sudden or gradual, the carpenter knew that he was no longer trustworthy—that is to say, he no longer cared whether people made trouble for one another or not. His wife saw that he looked tired, that he did not always bother to stand up straight, that he was beginning to show his age. And she tried to make his life easier for him, but he was a man firmly fixed in his habits, and there was not much she could do for him except feed him well and keep small irritations from him.

Out of habit, the carpenter continued not to repeat the things people told him, but while the secret was being handed over to him he marvelled that the other person had no suspicion he was making a mistake. And since the carpenter had not asked, after all, to be the repository of everybody's secret burden, it made him mildly resentful.

One day he tried an experiment. He betrayed a secret that was not very serious—partly to prove to himself that he could do such a thing and partly in the hope that word would get around that he was not to be trusted with secrets. It made a certain amount of trouble, as he knew it would, but it also had the effect of clearing the air for all concerned, and the blame never got back to him because no one could imagine his behaving in so uncharacteristic a fashion. So, after this experiment, he tried another. The butcher came in, closed the door softly, looked around for a pile of lumber to sit on, and then said, "There's something I've got to tell somebody."

"Don't tell me," the carpenter said quickly, "unless you want every Tom, Dick, and Harry to know."

The butcher paused, looked down at his terrible hands, cleared his throat, glanced around the shop, and then suddenly leaned forward and out it came.

"In short, he wanted every Tom, Dick, and Harry to know," the carpenter said to his wife afterward, when he was telling her about the butcher's visit.

"People need to make trouble the way they need to breathe," she said calmly.

"I don't need to make trouble," the carpenter said indignantly.

"I know," she said. "But you mustn't expect everyone to be like you."

The next time somebody closed the door softly and sat down and opened his mouth to speak, the carpenter beat him to it. "I know it isn't fair to tell you this," he said, "but I had to tell somebody . . ." This time he made quite a lot of trouble, but not so much that his wife couldn't deal with it, and he saw that the fear of making trouble can be worse than trouble itself.

After that, he didn't try any more experiments. What happened just happened. The candlemaker was sitting on a pile of lumber watching him saw a chestnut plank, and the carpenter said, "Yesterday the one-eyed fiddler was in here."

"Was he?" the candlemaker said; he wasn't really interested in the fiddler at that moment. There was something on his mind that he had to tell somebody, and he was waiting for the carpenter to stop sawing so he wouldn't have to raise his voice and run the risk of being overheard in the street.

"You know the blacksmith's little boy?" the carpenter said. "The second one? The one he keeps in the shop with him?"

"The apple of his eye," said the candlemaker. "Had him sorting nails when he was no bigger than a flea. Now he tends the bellows."

"That's right," said the carpenter. "Well, you know what the fiddler told me?"

"When it comes to setting everybody's feet a-dancing, there's no one like the one-eyed fiddler," the candlemaker said. "But I don't know what he'd of done without the blacksmith. Always taking him in when he didn't have a roof over his head or a penny in his pocket. Drunk or sober."

"You know what the fiddler told me? He said the blacksmith's little boy isn't his child."

"Whose is he?"

"Who does he look like?"

"Why, come to think of it, he looks like the one-eyed fiddler."

"Spitting image," the carpenter said. And not until that moment did he realize what was happening. It was the change in the candlemaker's face that made him aware of it. First the light of an impending confidence, which had been so clear in his eyes, was dimmed. The candlemaker looked down at his hands, which were as white and soft as a woman's. Then he cleared his throat and said, "Strange nobody noticed it."

"You won't tell anybody what I told you?" the carpenter found himself saying.

"No, of course not," the candlemaker said. "I always enjoy watching you work. Is that a new plane you've got there?"

For the rest of the visit he was more friendly than usual, as if some lingering doubt had been disposed of and he could now be wholly at ease with the carpenter. After he had gone, the carpenter started to use his new plane and it jammed. He cleaned the slot and adjusted the screw and blew on it, but it still jammed, so he put it aside, thinking the blade needed to be honed, and picked up a crosscut saw. Halfway through the plank he stopped. The saw was not following the pencil line. He gave up and sat down on a pile of lumber. The fiddler had better clear out now and never show his face in the village again, because if the blacksmith ever found out, he'd kill him. And what about the blacksmith's wife? She had no business doing what she did, but neither did the blacksmith have any business marrying someone young enough to be his daughter. She was a slight woman with a cough, and she wouldn't last a year if she had to follow the fiddler in and out of taverns and sleep under hedgerows. And what about the little boy who so proudly tended the bellows? Each question the carpenter asked himself was worse than the one before. His head felt heavy with shame. He sighed and then sighed again, deep heavy sighs forced out of him by the weight on his heart. How could he tell his wife what he had done? And what would make her want to go on living with him when she knew? And how could he live with himself? At last he got up and untied the strings of his apron and locked the door of his shop behind him and went off down the street, looking everywhere for the one-eyed fiddler.

12

The man who lost his father

ONCE upon a time there was a man who lost his father.
His father died of natural causes—that is to say,
illness and old age—and it was time for him to go, but
nevertheless the man was affected by it, more than he had
expected. He misplaced things: his keys, his reading glasses,
a communication from the bank. And he imagined things.
He imagined that his father's spirit walked the streets of
the city where he lived, was within touching distance of
him, could not for a certain time leave this world for
the world of spirits, and was trying to communicate with
him. When he picked up the mail that was lying on the
marble floor outside the door of his apartment, he expected to find a letter from his father telling him . . .
telling him what?

The secret of the After Life is nothing at all—or rather,
it is only one secret, compared to the infinite number of
secrets having to do with this life that the dead take with
them when they go.

"Why didn't I ask him when I had a chance?" the man
said, addressing the troubled face in the bathroom mirror, a

face made prematurely old by a white beard of shaving lather. And from that other mirror, his mind, the answer came: *Because you thought there was still time. You expected him to live forever . . . because you expect to live forever yourself.* The razor stopped in mid-stroke. This time what came was a question. *Do you or don't you? You do expect to live forever? You don't expect to live forever?* The man plunged his hands in soapy water and rinsed the lather from his face. And as he was drying his hands on a towel, he glanced down four stories at the empty street corner and for a split second he thought he saw his father, standing in front of the drugstore window.

His father's body was in a coffin, and the coffin was in the ground, in a cemetery, but that he never thought about. Authority is not buried in a wooden box. Nor safety (mixed with the smell of cigar smoke). Nor the firm handwriting. Nor the sound of his voice. Nor the right to ask questions that are painful to answer.

So long as his father was alive, he figured persistently in the man's conversation. Almost any remark was likely to evoke him. Although the point of the remark was mildly amusing and the tone intended to be affectionate, there was something about it that was not amusing and not entirely affectionate—as if an old grievance was still being nourished, a deep disagreement, a deprivation, something raked up out of the past that should have been allowed to lie forgotten. It was, actually, rather tiresome, but even after he perceived what he was doing the man could not stop. It made no difference whether he was with friends or with people he had never seen before. In the space of five minutes, his father would pop up in the conversation. And you didn't have to be very acute to understand that what he was really saying was "Though I am a grown man and not a little boy, I still feel the weight of my father's hand on me, and I tell this story to lighten the weight. . . ."

Now that his father was gone, he almost never spoke of him, but he thought about him. At my age was his hair this thin, the man wondered, holding his comb under the bathroom faucet.

Why, when he never went to church, did he change, the man wondered, dropping a letter in the corner mailbox. Why, when he had been an atheist, or if not an atheist then an agnostic, all his life, was he so pleased to see the Episcopal minister during his last illness?

Hanging in the hall closet was his father's overcoat, which by a curious accident now fit him. Authority had shrunk. And safety? There was no such thing as safety. It was only an idea that children have. As they think that with the help of an umbrella they can fly, so they feel that their parents stand between them and all that is dangerous. Meanwhile, the cleaning establishment had disposed of the smell of cigar smoke; the overcoat smelled like any overcoat. The handwriting on the envelopes he picked up in the morning outside his door was never that handwriting. And along with certain stock certificates that had been turned over to him when his father's estate was settled, he had received the right to ask questions that are painful to answer, such as "Why did you not value your youth?" and "Why is it you envy your father his friends?"

He wore the overcoat, which was of the very best quality but double-breasted and long and a dark charcoal gray —an old man's coat—only in very cold weather, and it kept him warm. . . . From the funeral home they went to the cemetery, and the coffin was already there, in a tent, suspended above the open grave. After the minister had spoken the last words, it still was not lowered. Instead, the mourners raised their heads, got up from their folding chairs, and went out into the icy wind of a January day. And to the man's surprise, the outlines of the bare trees were blurred. He had not expected tears, and neither had he expected to see, in a small group of people waiting some distance from the tent, a man and a woman, not related to each other and not married to each other, but both related to him: his first playmates. They stepped forward and took his hand and spoke to him, looking deeply into his eyes. The only possible conclusion was that they were there waiting for him, in the cold, because they were worried about him. . . . In his father's end was his own beginning, the mirror in his mind pointed out. And it was true, in more ways than one. But it took time.

H E let go of the ghost in front of the corner drugstore. The questions grew less and less painful to have to answer. The stories he told his children about their grandfather did not have to do with a disagreement, a deprivation, or something raked up out of the distant past that might better have been forgotten. When he was abrupt with them and they ran crying from the room, he thought, *But my voice wasn't all that harsh.* Then he thought, *To them it must have been.* And he got up from his chair and went after them, to lighten the weight of his father's irritability, making itself felt in some mysterious way through him. They forgave him, and he forgave his father, who surely hadn't meant to sound severe and unloving. And when he took his wife and children home—to the place that in his childhood was home—on a family visit, one of his cousins, smiling, said "How much like your father you are."

"That's because I am wearing his overcoat," the man
said—or rather, the child that survived in the man. The
man himself was pleased, accepted the compliment (surpris-
ing though it was), and at the first opportunity looked in
the mirror to see if it was true.

13

The industrious tailor

ONCE upon a time, in the west of England, there
was an industrious tailor who was always sitting
cross-legged, plying his needle, when the sun came up
over the hill, and all day long he drove himself, as if
he were beating a donkey with a stick. "I am almost
through cutting out this velvet waistcoat," he would tell
himself, "and when I am through cutting the velvet, I will
cut the yellow satin lining. And then there is the buckram,
and the collar and cuffs. The cuffs are to be thirteen inches
wide, tapering to ten and a half—his lordship was very
particular about that detail—and faced with satin. The
basting should take me into the afternoon, and if all goes
well, and I don't see why it shouldn't, I ought to be able to
do all twenty-seven buttonholes before the light gives
out."

When snow lay deep on the ground and the sheep stayed
in their pens, the shepherd came down to the tavern and in
the conviviality he found there made up for the months of
solitude on the moors. During the early part of the summer, when it was not yet time for anybody to be bringing
wheat, barley, and rye to the mill to be ground into flour,

the miller got out his hook and line and went fishing. In one way or another, everyone had some time that he called his own. On the first of May, lads and lasses went into the wood just before daybreak and came back wearing garlands of flowers and with their arms around each other. From his window the tailor saw them setting up the Maypole, but he did not lay aside his needle and thread and go join in the dancing. It is true that he was no longer young and, with his bald head and his bent back and his solemn manner, would have looked odd dancing around a Maypole, but that did not deter the miller's wife, who weighed seventeen stone and was as light on her feet as a fairy and didn't care who laughed at her as long as she was enjoying herself.

When the industrious tailor came to the end of all the work that he could expect for a while and his worktable was quite bare, he looked around for some lily that needed gilding. Sorting his pins, sharpening his scissors, and rearranging his patterns, he congratulated himself on keeping busy, though he might just as well have been sitting in his doorway enjoying the sun, for his scissors didn't need sharpening, and his patterns were not in disorder, and a pin is a pin, no matter what tray you put it in.

As with all of us, the tailor's upbringing had a good deal to do with the way he behaved. At the age of eight, he was apprenticed to his father, who was a master tailor and not only knew all there is to know about making clothes but also was full of native wisdom. While the boy was learning to sew a straight seam and how to cut cloth on the diagonal and that sort of thing, the father would from time to time raise his right hand, with the needle and thread in it, and, looking at the boy over the top of his spectacles, say "A stitch in time saves nine," or "Waste makes want," or some other bit of advice, which the boy took to his bosom and cherished. And he had never forgotten a wonderful story his father told about an ant and a grasshopper. Of all his father's sayings, the one that made the deepest impression on him was "Never put off till tomorrow what you can do today," though as a rule the industrious tailor had already done it yesterday and was hard at work on something that did not need to be done until the day after.

WHAT is true of the day after tomorrow is equally true of the day after that, and the day after that, and the day after that, and so on, and in time a very curious thing happened. There was the past—there is always the past—and it was full of accomplishment, of things done well before they needed to be done, and the tailor regarded it with satisfaction. And there was the future, when things would have to be done, and bills would have to be made out and respectfully submitted and paid or not paid, as the case might be, and new work would be ordered, and so on. But it was never right now. The present had ceased to exist. When the industrious tailor looked out of the window and saw that it was raining, it was not raining today but on a day in the middle of next week, or the week after that, if he was that far ahead of himself, and he often was. You would have thought that he would sooner or later have realized that the time he was spending so freely was next month's, and that if he had already lived through the days of this month before it was well begun he was living beyond his means. But what is "already"? What is "now"? The words had lost their meaning. And this was not as serious as it sounds, because words are, after all, only words. "I could kill you for doing that," a man says to his wife and then they both cheerfully sit down to dinner. And many people live entirely in the past, without even noticing it. One day the tailor pushed his glasses up on his forehead and saw that he was in the middle of a lonely wood. He rubbed his poor tired eyes, but the trees didn't go away. He looked all around. No scissors and pins, no bolts of material, no patterns, no worktable, no shop. Only the needle and thread he had been sewing with. He listened anxiously. He had never been in a wood before. "Wife?" he called out, but there was no answer.

He knew that it was late afternoon, and that he ought to get out of the wood before dark, so he stuck the needle in his vest and started walking along a path that constantly threatened to disappear, the way paths do in a wood. Sometimes the path divided, and he had to choose between the right and the left fork, without knowing which was the way that led out of the wood. The light began to fail even sooner than he had expected. When it was still daytime in the sky overhead, it was already so dark where he was that he could find the path only by the feel of the ground under his feet.

"I don't see why this should happen to me," he said, and from the depths of the wood a voice said "To *who?*" disconcertingly, but it was only an owl. So he kept on until he saw a light through the trees, and he made his way to it, through the underbrush and around fallen logs, until he came to a house in a clearing. At this time of night they'll be easily frightened, he thought. I must speak carefully or they'll close the door in my face. When the door opened in answer to his knock and a woman stood looking out at him from the lighted doorway, he said politely, "It's all right, ma'am, I'm not a robber."

"No," the woman said, "you're an industrious tailor."

"Now, how did you know that?" he asked in amaze-ment.

The woman did not seem to feel that this question needed answering, and there was something about her that made him uneasy, and so, though he would much rather that she invited him in and gave him a place by the fire and a bit of supper, he said, "If you would be kind enough to show me the way out of the wood—"

"I don't know that I can," the woman said.

"Isn't there a road of some kind?"

"There's a road," the woman said doubtfully, "but it wasn't built in your lifetime."

"I beg pardon?"

"And anyway, you'd soon lose it in the dark. You'll have to wait until morning. How did you happen to—"

At that point a baby began to cry, and the woman said, "I can't stand here talking. Come in."

"Thank you," he said. "That's very kind of you, ma'am," and as he stepped across the threshold there was suddenly no house, no lighted room, no woman. Nothing but a clearing in the wood.

In disappointment so acute that it brought tears to his eyes, he sat down on the ground and tucked his legs under him and tried to get used to the idea that he wasn't going to sit by a warm fire, under a snug roof, with a bit of supper by and by, and a place to lay his head at bedtime.

I will catch my death of pneumonia, he thought. He put his hand to his vest; the needle was still there. He felt his forehead, and then took his glasses off, folded them care-fully, and put them in his vest pocket. Then he stretched out on the bare ground and, looking up through the trees, thought about his tailor shop, and about a greatcoat that he was working on. It was of French blue, part true cashmere and part Lincoln wool, with a three-tiered cape, and it wasn't promised until a fortnight, but he would have finished it and have given it to his wife to press if he hadn't suddenly found himself in this lonely wood. Then he thought about his wife, who would be wondering why he didn't come upstairs for his supper. And then about his father, who had a stroke and never recovered the use of his limbs or his speech. In the evening, after the day was over, the industrious tailor used to come and sit by his father's bed, and he would bring whatever he was working on—a waistcoat or a pair of knee breeches, or an embroidered vest—and spread it out on the counterpane, to show his father that the lessons had been well learned and that he needn't worry about the quality of work being turned out by the shop. And instead of being pleased with him, his father would push the work aside impatiently. There seemed to be something on his mind that he very much wanted to say, some final piece of wisdom, but when he tried to speak he could only utter meaningless sounds.

Now, through the tops of the bare trees, the tailor could see the stars, so bright and so far away . . . But how did it get to be autumn, he wondered. And why am I not cold? Why am I not hungry? He fell asleep and dreamed that he had more work to do than he could possibly manage, and woke up with the sun shining in his face.

"Wife?" he called out, before he remembered where he was or what had happened to him.

He sat up and looked around. There was no house in the clearing, and no sign that there ever had been, but there was a path leading off through the woods, and he followed it. At this time, more than half of England was forests, and so he knew that it might be days before he found his way out of the wood. "I must be careful not to walk in a circle," he told himself. "That's what people always do when they are lost." But one fallen tree, one sapling, one patch of dried fern, one bed of moss looked just like another, and he could not tell whether he was walking in a circle or not. Now and then, not far from the path, there would be a sudden dry rustle that made his heart race. Was it a poisonous viper? What was it? The rustle did not explain itself. Oddly enough, he himself, stepping on dry leaves and twigs, did not make a sound.

"I ought to be living on roots and berries," he said to himself, and though there were plenty of both, he did not know which were edible and which were not, and he did not feel inclined to experiment. But when he came to a spring, he thought, I will drink, because this far from any house or pasture it cannot be contaminated. . . . He knelt down and put his face to the water and nothing happened. His throat was as dry as before. The water remained just out of reach. He leaned farther forward and again nothing happened. The water kept receding until his face touched dry gravel. He raised his head in surprise and there was the beautiful spring, glittering, jewel-like in the sunlight, pushing its way under logs and between boulders, murmuring as it went, but not to be drunk from. "Can it be that I am dead?" the tailor asked himself. And then, "If I am dead, why has nobody told me where to go, or what's expected of me?"

As he walked on, he tried to remember if in the old days, before he suddenly found himself in this wood, he had ever got down on his hands and knees to drink from a spring. All he remembered was that when the other boys were roaming the woods and bathing in the river, he was in his father's shop learning to be a master tailor.

"It is possible that I am dreaming," he said to himself.

But it did not seem like a dream. In dreams it is always—not twilight exactly, but the light is peculiar, comes from nowhere, and is never very bright. This was a blindingly beautiful sunny day.

"At all events," he said to himself, "I am a much better walker than I had any idea. I have been walking for hours and I don't feel in the least tired. And even if it should turn out that I have been walking in a circle—"

At that moment he saw, ahead of him, what seemed like a thinning out of trees, as if he was coming to the edge of the wood. It proved to be a small clearing with a house in it. Smoke was rising from the chimney, and as the tailor came nearer an unpleasant suspicion cross his mind.

"Oh, it's you," the woman said, when she opened the door and saw him standing there. She had a baby in her arms, and she didn't look particularly pleased to see him, or concerned that he had passed the whole night on the bare ground and the whole day walking in a circle.

"I'm sorry to trouble you, ma'am," he said, "but if you will be so kind as to show me that road you were speaking of—"

The baby began to fret, and the woman jounced it lightly on her shoulder. "As you can see, I'm busy," she said. "And I don't see how you got here in the first place."

"Neither do I," he said.

"Did you come on a spring anywhere in the wood?"

He nodded.

"And did you drink from it?"

"I couldn't," he said. "When I put my face to the water, there wasn't any."

"I'm afraid there's nothing I can do," the woman said, and he saw that she was about to close the door in his face.

"Please, ma'am," he said, "if you'll just show me where that road begins I won't trouble you any further, I promise you."

"Why you had to come today of all days, when the baby's cutting a tooth, and the fire in the stove has gone out, and I still have to do the churning. . . . You haven't murdered somebody? No, I can see you haven't. If the police are after you—"

"The police are not after me," the tailor said with dignity, "and I haven't committed any crime that I know of."

"Well, that doesn't mean anything," the woman said. "Come, let me show you the road."

He followed her across the clearing, and when she stopped they were standing in front of a clump of white birch trees. Beyond it the tangled underbrush began, and the big trees.

"I don't see any road," the tailor said.

"That's what I mean," the woman said. She stood looking at him and frowning thoughtfully.

"Even if there was only a path—" the tailor began, and the woman said, "Oh, be quiet. If I let you go off into the woods again, you'll only end up here the way you did before. And I can't ask you into the house, because—Have you ever held a baby?"

"Oh, yes," the tailor said. "My children are grown now, but when they were little I often held them while my wife was busy doing something."

As he was speaking, the woman put the baby in his arms. The baby turned its head on its weak neck and looked at him. Though the woman made him uneasy, the baby did not. The baby's face contorted, and he saw that it was about to cry. "Hush-a," he said, and jounced it gently against his shoulder, and felt the head wobble against his neck, and the down on the baby's head, softer than any material in his shop.

"This may not work," the woman said, and started back across the clearing, and he followed her, still holding the baby.

At the door of the house she took a firm grip on the hem of the baby's garment and then she said, "Go in, go in," and after a last look over his shoulder at the clearing in the wood he stepped across the threshold, expecting to find himself outside again, and instead he was in his own shop, sitting cross-legged on his worktable.

H E listened and heard the twittering of birds as they flitted from branch to branch in the elm tree outside, and then the miller's wife, laughing at some joke she had just made. He saw by the quality of the light outside that it was only the middle of the afternoon. A wagon came by, and the miller's wife called to whoever was in the wagon, and a man's voice said, "Whoa, there ... Whoa ... Whoa." The tailor listened with rapt attention to the conversation that followed, though he had heard it a hundred times. Or conversations just like it. All around him on the worktable were scraps of French-blue material, and he could see at a glance what was waiting to be stitched to what. Finally the man said, "That's rich! That's a good one. Gee-up ..." and the wheels turned again, and the slow plodding was resumed and grew fainter and was replaced by the sound of a child beating on a tin pan. The miller's wife went home, but there were other sounds—a dog, a door slamming, a child being scolded. Then it was quiet for a time, and without thinking the tailor put his hand to his vest and found the needle. Two boys went by, saying, "I dare you to do it,

I dare you, I double-dare you!" Do what, the tailor wondered, and went on sewing.

The quiet and the outbreaks of sound alternated in a way that was so regular that it almost seemed planned. A loud noise, such as a crow going caw, caw, caw, seemed to produce a deeper silence afterward. He studied the beautiful sound of footsteps approaching and receding, so like a piece of music.

The light began to fail and he hardly noticed it, because as the light went it was accompanied by all the sounds that mean the end of the day: men coming home from the fields, shops being closed, children being called in before dark.

When the tailor could not see any longer, he put his work aside and sat, listening and smiling to himself at what he heard, until his wife called him to supper.

14

The woman with a talent for talking

IN the very olden times, in a village that was a whole day's march from the main road that led from Athens to Thebes, there was a woman who differed from her neighbors in that she seemed to have no special talent that reflected credit on her. As she continually observed, each of them had some accomplishment at which they so far excelled her and everyone else that there was no point in trying to match them. "I have a fool-proof receipt for stewing a kid in white wine," she would say to herself, "but what is the use of my trying to make appetizing meals when Cleome cooks by instinct, without ever looking at a receipt? . . . I could raise parsley and sage and sweet marjoram and basil and lavender, like Dido, but that takes a well-drained soil and a green thumb, neither of which I happen to have, and you have to be outdoors all day, and how would I get the weaving done? The weaving is more important. . . . Dorcas has been weaving since she was a child. Her mother taught her to weave, and now her cloth is fine and even throughout, whereas mine puckers. She doesn't even have to look while she weaves. Her hands do it for her. As for cutting the cloth that Dorcas weaves so beautifully, I could never do that as well as Sappho, who looks at her husband and cuts out a cloak that hangs from his shoulders the way the woodbine hangs from the oak. . . ."

So the woman considered and rejected the knacks and skills she saw all around her, and the more discontented with herself she became, the more she was compelled to communicate her dissatisfaction to someone, and so she went from house to house, saying, as she opened the door, "With all there is to do at home, I really shouldn't be here. What's that you're doing?" And they showed her what they were doing, and she was full of genuine admiration, which she had to express, being of an enthusiastic disposition, and then the cork was out of the bottle. For the woman did have a talent, and it was for talking. At first the other women wasted their time trying to get a word in now and then, which was barely possible and not worth the effort, because the woman whose talent was for talking had no more talent for listening than she had for weaving. Or they put aside their work, hoping that if they gave her their full attention, she would shortly leave them in peace. She didn't leave them in peace. Having admired what they were doing, she sat down in a nice comfortable chair and began to tell them what she was thinking of doing, and whatever it was, they knew from past experience that she was never going to get around to doing it, and it took real strength of character not to point this out to her. So they picked up their work again, and without meaning to, they stopped listening to her—except for a word now and then —and she didn't care whether they listened to her or not, so long as they allowed her to give voice to every stray thought that crossed her continually straying mind. She not only told them what she thought and how she felt about everything, but how they felt and what they thought. This she caught out of the air. Her talent was quite out of her control, like her tongue, and what she told them was, on the whole, accurate enough. It dramatized their monotonous lives, and relieved the feelings of those who were encouraging water to run uphill or trying to make a silk purse out of a sow's ear or remaining silent in circumstances where silence is golden. After she left, they went about their work serenely and did not provoke their husbands or scold their children or beat the kitchen maid.

For many years the village lived in something like harmony, far from the main road that led from Athens to Thebes, until one morning a stranger passed through the marketplace—a mischievous-looking young man with a white cloak, gilt sandals with little wings on them, a grey dove on his shoulder, and an oak staff in his hand. The stranger and the woman with the talent for talking met and fell into conversation at the well. That is to say, she talked and he listened intently to everything she had to say. After a time they left the well and sat on the steps of the Temple of War. After a time they left the Temple of War and sat on the steps of the Temple of Wisdom. After a time they left the Temple of Wisdom and sat on the steps of the Temple of Love. After a time they left the Temple of Love and went into the woman's house, and when night came the stranger was still there. When he left no one knew, but he was gone when the woman's husband came home driving his goats ahead of him.

A whole day and a whole night passed, and by the next morning the women of the village had become aware that something was wrong. One by one, they paused in the midst of their work and looked at one another and said,

"Have you talked to Oenone? I didn't see her all day yesterday." No one had seen her. So they stopped what they were doing and went to her house. The floor was unswept, the cooking pots were unwashed, the cat was complaining. This was not unusual, any of it. What was unusual was the silence. They called and got no answer. And finally they peered into the room where the woman and her husband slept, on a bed that was seldom made before dark, and there she lay, with her eyes wide open and the cover drawn up to her chin.

THAT evening when the woman's husband came home from the hills, the other women were waiting for him. It had been a trying day, and they were cross as bears. "What's happened?" they demanded. "Is Oenone sick? Is she just too tired to get out of bed? Is she discouraged with life?"

"All I know," he said sadly, "is what she said in her sleep."

He started to turn and go into the house, but they stopped him.

"Tell us," they said. "What did Oenone say in her sleep?"

"It is of no consequence," he said. "And I don't know that she would like me to repeat things that she does not know she said."

The women swore they would not tell a living soul, and, looking around, he saw that there was not much likelihood of their telling anybody because they were all here, so he said, "It sounded like 'The stranger!'"

"And then?" the women said.

"That's all she said."

"Well, that's very interesting," Penelope said, "as far as it goes. But meanwhile, I cannot thread my needle, I am so confused and irritable."

"I'm sick of weaving," Dorcas said. "Even though I do it better than anybody else. Other women can move about while they are working, but I am chained to this loom."

"It is discouraging to have to cook with dried herbs that have lost most of their savor," Cleome said, "when I know that if I only had time—Oenone has often told me that if I only had time I could raise my own herbs like Dido, and pick a leaf or two fresh from the garden as I needed them."

"The garden," Dido said, "takes all my energy and prevents me from learning to play the flute, as Oenone wants me to do."

Because Oenone was not there to weave these complaints into her conversation and so dispose of them, dissatisfaction hung over the village like a cloud of devouring insects.

This situation lasted for two more days, and on the third night the woman once more cried out in her sleep. Now, to people who talk in their sleep all questions are a warning, and so the woman's husband was careful to speak only in statements. "Yes," he said quietly and evenly. "The dreadful stranger."

"He said—" the woman began.

"He said something," the man prompted.

"He said nothing," the woman said in her sleep. "That was what was so dreadful. If he had said anything, I would still be talking. But he was silent, and it was growing dark outside, and it came to me out of the air that he was a god and knew what I was thinking, and that I didn't need to say it out loud. The reason I talk is—"

The man waited.

"The reason I talk," the woman said, moaning, "is that there is something I don't want to say. I don't know what it is. I only know that if I hear myself saying it, something dreadful will happen."

"I see," the man said, in a voice hardly above a whisper. "I could be wrong, of course, but I always thought you did not listen to what you were saying."

"No," the woman said in her sleep, "I do not listen. I do not want to listen. If I did, I would catch nothing out of the air."

"I am with the goats all day and sometimes all night, and they never say anything but bla-aa, and so I am out of the habit of listening—to them, or myself, or you. And Dorcas and Sappho and Cleome and Dido and Hermione do not listen because they are too involved in their own affairs."

"That's true," the woman said, and fell into a deep sleep.

In the morning, she woke in her usual cheerful frame of mind and went about her talking. Wherever she appeared, the women were too busy to stop and listen to her, and a great deal was accomplished. The seedlings were thinned, the knitting grew longer and longer, the dough was kneaded and set to rise, the soiled clothes were washed on the riverbank. Toward nightfall, the woman heard a dove calling from the edge of the wood, and interrupted herself to listen uneasily. But common sense told her, and she told the person she was talking to, that any interest the gods take in the lives of mortals must be fleeting. By and by, having been everywhere else, she went home, fully intending to cook her husband a good supper, and found that he had eaten long since, and was keeping her plate warm by the fire.

15

The man who took his family to the seashore

ONCE upon a time there was a man who took his family to the seashore. They had a cottage on the ocean, and it was everything that a house by the ocean should be—sagging wicker furniture, faded detective stories, blue china, grass rugs, other people's belongings to reflect upon, and other people's pots and pans to cook with. The first evening, after the children were in bed, the man and his wife sat on the porch and watched the waves come in as if they had never seen this sight before. It was a remarkably beautiful evening, no wind, and a calm sea. Far out on the broad back of the ocean a hump would begin to gather slowly, moving toward the shore, and at a certain point the hump would rise in a dark wall and spill over. A sandpiper went skittering along the newly wetted, shining sand, the beach grass all leaned one way, the moon was riding high and white in the evening sky, and wave after wave broke just before it reached the shore. The woman said to the man, "What are you thinking about?"

"I was thinking about how many waves there are," he said, which made her laugh.

"Thousands upon thousands," he said solemnly. "Millions . . . Billions . . ."

He had been brought up far inland, where the only water was a pond or a creek winding its way through marshes and pastures, and though this was not his first time at the ocean, he could not get over it. No duck pond has ever yet gathered itself into a dark wall of water. Creeks gurgle and swirl between their muddy banks, but never succeed in producing anything like the ocean's lisp and roar. There was nothing to compare it to except itself.

The next morning he went for a swim before breakfast. The waves were high, but he waited, and the moment came when he could run in and swim out into deep water. He swam until he was tired, and then rode in on a wave, and dried himself, and went back to the house with a huge appetite.

There was no newspaper to remind him that it was now Sunday the twentieth, and that tomorrow would be Monday the twenty-first. There was a clock in the kitchen, but he seldom looked at it, and his watch lay in his bureau drawer with the hands resting at one-fifteen. The only thing that kept him from feeling that time was standing still was the sound that came through the open windows: *Sish . . . sish . . . sish . . . sish . . . a-wish . . . sish . . .*

As always when people are at the ocean, the years fell away. The crow's-feet around the man's eyes remained white longer than the rest of his face, and then all the wrinkles were smoothed away during the nights of deep sleep and the days of idleness. He and his wife were neither of them young, and nothing could bring back the look of really being young, but five, ten, fifteen years fell off them. When they made love their bodies tasted of the salt sea, and when the wave of lovemaking had spent itself, they lay in one another's arms, and heard the sound of the waves. This year, and next year, and last year, and the year before that, and the year after next, and before they came, and after they had gone. . . .

The woman was afraid of the surf, and would not go past a certain point, though he coaxed her to join him. She stood timidly, this side of the breaking waves, and he left her after a while and went out past the sandy foam, to where he could stand and dive through the incoming wall of water. There was always the moment of decision, and this was what she dreaded, and why she remained on the shore—because the moment came when you had to decide and she couldn't decide. Years ago she had been rolled, and the fright had never left her. So had he, of course. He remembered what it had been like, and knew that if he wasn't careful diving through the waves he would be whipped around and lose control of what happened to him, and his face would be ground into the sharp gravel at the water's edge, his bathing trunks would be filled with sand, and, floundering and frightened, he would barely be able to struggle to his feet in time to keep it from happening all over again. But he was careful. He kept his eyes always on the incoming wave, and, swimming hard for a few seconds, he suddenly found himself safe on the other side. As he came out of the water, his face was transformed with happiness. He took the towel his wife held out to him and, hopping on one leg, to shake the water out of his ears, he said, "This is the way I remember feeling when I was seventeen years old."

While she was shopping for food he went into the post office and waited while a girl with sun-bleached hair sorted through a pile of envelopes. He came away with several, including a bank statement, which he looked at, out of habit—debits and credits, the brief but furious struggle between incoming salary and outgoing expenses—and then put in the same drawer with his watch.

All through sunny days, and cloudy days, and days when it rained, and days when the fog rolled in from the ocean and shut out the sight of the neighboring houses, the waves broke, and broke, and broke, always with the same drawn-out sound, and silently the days dropped from the calendar. The vacation was half over. Then there were only ten more days. Then it was the last Sunday, the last Monday. . . . Sitting up in bed, the man saw that there was a path of bright moonlight across the water, which the incoming waves passed through, and the moonlight made it seem as if you could actually see the earth's curve.

During the final week there were two days in a row when the sky was racked with storm clouds, and it rained intermittently, and the red flag flew from the pole by the lifeguard's stand, and only the young dared go in. Like dolphins sporting, the man thought as he stood on the beach, fully dressed, with a windbreaker on, and watched the teen-agers diving through the cliffs of water. The waves went *crash!* and then *crash!* and again *crash!* all night long.

This stormy period was followed by a day when the ocean was like a millpond, and the waves were so small they hardly got up enough hump to spill over, but spill over they did. *Sish . . . sish . . . a-wish . . .* Since the world began, he thought, stretched out on his beach towel. The I.B.M. machine had not been invented that could enumerate them. It would be like counting the grains of sand all up and down the miles and miles of beach. It would take forever. He could not stop thinking about it, and he decided that in a way it was worse than being rolled.

It was what reconciled him, in the end, to the packing and the last time for this and the last time for that, and getting dressed in city clothes, and the melancholy ritual of departure. It was too much. The whole idea was more than the mind could manage. Outside the human scale. Rather than think about the true number of the waves, he gave up his claim to the shore they broke upon, and the beach grass all leaning one way, and the moon's path across the water, and the illusion that he could actually see the earth's curve.

From the deck of the ferryboat that took them across the bay to the mainland, he watched the island grow smaller and smaller. And in two weeks' time he had forgotten all about what it was like, *this year . . . next year . . . last year . . . and before we came . . . and after we've gone . . .*

16

The woman who didn't want anything more

ONCE upon a time there was a woman who didn't
want anything more. Tables, chairs, pictures, old
china, potted plants, scatter rugs, washcloths, bookends,
sewing scissors—there was nothing she needed beyond
what she already had, and when people asked her "Isn't
there something you'd like for your birthday?" she said
"No, I really don't want a thing," which bothered them,
of course, because there were a great many things that
they wanted, and so they set about trying to find something for her. They gave her cookbooks, which she
thanked them for politely and put on the shelf with the
other cookbooks. They gave her hooked rugs, which she
thanked them for and put in the attic. They gave her
autographed copies of their own books, which she had already bought and read, but she thanked them and put the
two copies side by side in the bookcase. They gave her
woollen scarves, which had to be wrapped in newspaper
and put away in the cedar chest, which was full. And they
gave her a portable television set, a footstool, a fire screen,
and a folding table, all of which presented a problem to

her, though she managed eventually to put them away somewhere out of sight.

"If people only wouldn't give me things," she used to say to herself, without realizing for quite a long while that she had gone one step further and didn't even want the things she already had.

One day, she opened her front door, with her hat and coat and gloves on, ready to go out and get in the car and drive downtown, and there, lying across the welcome mat, was a man, sound asleep or dead drunk, she was not sure which. His clothes were filthy, he needed a bath, and he hadn't shaved, and it was obvious at a glance that he was a tramp, with nothing in his pockets, and no place of his own to go to.

Her first impulse was to step back into the house and call the police, but then he opened his eyes, which were so mild in their expression that she had another impulse instead, which was to go back inside and make him a pot of coffee. And then she had the third and most interesting idea of all.

She opened her purse and took out her house key and her car key and gave them to him. On second thought, she handed him her purse, too, and went off down the sidewalk without looking back to see what happened.

If she had stopped to think, she would have realized that you don't get rid of everything you own as easily as all that. She should have given him a deed to the house, and the registration certificate for the car, and a forwarding address to show to people who turned up asking for her, and a signed statement to show to the police. But she didn't think of any of these things, because she was so taken with the idea of giving away everything she had, three days before Christmas, when the hall closet was full of unopened packages and the mailman came twice a day with more.

There was snow on the ground, but she had her arctics on, and it did not occur to her to give them away, because she was not morbid or fanatical. She walked downtown, and tried not to see the store windows, which usually depressed her because they were full of things she already had, or had had until a few minutes ago, and one does not get used to the idea of being free of things all at once; it takes time. The people she passed were carrying all sorts of awkward parcels, sometimes two and three of them tied together, and these things they had bought and were carrying home, either to give to somebody or to give to themselves, did not seem to have brought the light of pleasure to their eyes. She came to a bakery, and the sight of the Italian fruit bread and French pastries and *croissants* and *brioches* and hard-crusted wheels and sticks of white bread in the window reminded her that there was no bread in the house. She didn't want any for herself; she was not hungry. But she remembered the tramp, who would probably be disappointed when he sat down at the kitchen table with a cup of hot coffee and found there was no bread and butter to go with it. So she turned and went into the shop, which was crowded with people buying bread and pastry and party favors and other fancy staples for the holidays, but she didn't mind waiting. There was nothing that she should have been doing at that moment, and the place smelled of fresh bread, which was baked on the premises, and it was a long time since she had smelled this happy smell.

When her turn came, she got as far as "I want—" and then stopped, because her arm was unnaturally light without the familiar weight of her purse on it. But she realized that the tramp could—and in fact would have to—go out

and buy his own bread, because she had given him all the
money she had, and her bankbook, in case he ran out of
cash, which he eventually would, and needed to dip into
her savings account. So, smiling at the woman behind the
counter, she said, "I just want to stand here and smell the
smell of fresh bread."

Unfortunately, there were a great many things that the
woman behind the counter wanted, and so she didn't understand; besides, she had grown so accustomed to the smell of
fresh bread that she didn't even smell it any more. And she
suspected that the woman was a thief, or perhaps the ac-
complice of thieves, who, when she signalled to them that
the shop was empty of customers, would rush in, with their
faces masked and guns in their hands, and help themselves
to the contents of the cash register. But if you are in business you never can be sure who you are dealing with, and
one person's money is as good as another's, and so she
pointed to a sign: "No loitering on the Premises."

"I see," said the woman, and turned and went outside. It
was getting dark, and she had no place to go to, which
pleased her, and no engagements, which also pleased her,
but she found that she couldn't get the smell of fresh bread
out of her mind as she walked along, with her collar turned
up against the evening wind. Suddenly it occurred to her
that she could go back home—only it was not her home
any longer—and ask the tramp if he'd mind if she made
some bread.

THE front door was wide open and the oil-burner was
running. The key was in the door. She called and there
was no answer. The place, which she had expected to
find ransacked from top to bottom, seemed to be in per-

fect order, except that the car keys were lying on the
floor in the library. She saw, looking out of the library
window, that the car was still in the garage. Nothing
was missing: not the contents of her purse, which she
did not want; not the typewriter, which she seldom used;
not the portable TV, which she never turned on; not
the pair of expensive binoculars somebody had insisted on
giving her; not even the flat silver and her jewelry, which
she would have been happy to see the last of. Apparently,
the man she found lying on her doorstep didn't want anything either. With a deep sigh, she adjusted herself to the
idea that she was not, after all, free of things, and with a
shrug accepted the idea that she still had a roof over her
head. "I wonder if he—" she said to herself, and started for
the kitchen, which was in some disorder. The tramp had
not stopped to make a pot of coffee for himself, but had
sampled the contents of the liquor closet instead, and then
worked his way rather unsystematically through the ice-
box, tossing wrappers and bones and anything in the way
of leftovers that didn't appeal to him on the kitchen floor.
"Surely he wouldn't think to—" the woman said to herself
hopefully, and with a beating heart she put out her hand
and opened the flour bin. Sure enough, the tramp had not
stolen the flour; or, it turned out, the skim milk, or the
butter, or the yeast, or the salt and sugar.

She got out the breadboard and the measuring spoons
and the measuring cups, and put on a clean white apron,
and began to measure and mix the ingredients, and when
the dough had risen and the oven was the right temperature, she slipped the pans in and closed the oven door
quickly and sat down to wait. For a short while she was
afraid that the whole thing was an illusion, and that she
would not really care any more about the smell of fresh

bread baking than she did about hooked rugs there was no floor space for, or the woollen scarves in the cedar chest, or the money in her savings account, or the roof over her head. Then it began, faintly, ever so faintly at first, but unmistakable. She closed her eyes and caught the odor with a series of little searching sniffs.

"*Oh, bread, hurry!*" she said to it, and when the bread, all golden, was out of the pans and cooling on the kitchen table, she made herself a pot of good strong coffee. This is more like it, she said to herself. And indeed, from that time on, it was.

17

The kingdom where straightforward, logical thinking was admired over every other kind

IN a kingdom somewhere between China and the Caucasus, it became so much the fashion to admire straightforward, logical thinking over every other kind that the inhabitants would not tolerate any angle except a right angle or any line that was not the shortest distance between two points. All the pleasant meandering roads were straightened, which meant that a great many comfortable old houses had to be demolished and people were often obliged to drive miles out of their way to get to their destination. Fruit trees were pruned so that their branches went straight out or straight up, and stopped bearing fruit. Babies were made to walk at nine months—with braces, if necessary. Elderly persons could not be bent with age. All anybody has to do is look around to see that Nature is partial to curves and irregularities, but it was considered vulgar to look anywhere but straight ahead. The laws of the land reflected the universal prejudice. An accused person was quickly found to be innocent or guilty, and if there were any extenuating circumstances, the judge did not want to hear about them.

In the fiftieth year of his reign the old king, who was much loved, met with an accident. Looking straight ahead instead of where he was putting his feet, he walked into a charcoal burner's pit and broke his neck. The new king was every bit as inflexible as his father, and after he ascended the throne things should have gone exactly as before, only they never do. The king had only one child. The Princess Horizon was as beautiful as the first hour of a summer day, and the common people believed that fairies had attended her christening. Her manner with the greatest lord of the land and with the poorest peasant was the same—graceful, simple, and direct. She was intelligent but not too intelligent, proud but not haughty, and skillful at terminating conversations. She was everything that a princess should be. But she was also something a princess should not be. Or to put it differently, there was a flaw in her character, though it would not have been considered a flaw in yours or mine. Because of the royal blood in her veins, it wasn't suitable for her to be alone, from the moment she woke, in a room full of expectant courtiers, until it was time for her to close her eyes to all the flattery around her and go to sleep. But when the Princess' ladies-in-waiting had finished grouping themselves about her chair and were ready to take up their embroidery, they would discover that the chair was empty. How she had managed to elude them they could not imagine and the chair did not say. Or they would precede her, in the order of their rank, down some long, mirrored gallery, only to find when they reached the end of it that there was no one behind them. When she should have been opening a charity bazaar she was exercising her pony; someone else had to judge the

footraces and award the blue ribbon for the largest vegetable and the smallest stitches. When she should have been
laying a cornerstone she was climbing some remote tower
of the palace, hoping to find an old woman with a spindle.
When she should have been sitting in the royal box at the
opera, showing off the Crown jewels and encouraging the
Arts, she was in some empty maid's room reading a book.
And when the royal family appeared on a balcony reserved
for historical occasions and bowed graciously to the cheering multitudes, the Princess Horizon was conspicuously ab-
sent. All this was duly reported in the sealed letters the
foreign ambassadors sent home to their respective mon-
archs, and it no doubt explains why there were no offers
for her hand in marriage, though she was beautiful and
accomplished and everything a Princess should be.

One summer afternoon, the ladies-in-waiting, having
searched everywhere for her, departed in a string of carriages, and shortly afterward the Princess let herself out by
a side door and hurried off to the English garden. She was
in a doleful mood, and felt like reciting poetry. Everywhere else in the world at the time, English gardens were
by careful cultivation made to look wild, romantic, and
uncultivated. This English garden was laid out according
to the cardinal points of the compass. Even so, it was more
informal than the French and Italian gardens, which were
like nothing so much as a lesson in plane geometry. Addressing the empty afternoon, the Princess began:

> "The wind blows out; the bubble dies;
> The spring entombed in autumn dies;
> The dew dries up; the star is shot;
> The flight is past; and man—"

At that moment she observed something so strange she

thought she must be dreaming. A small white rosebush named after the Queen of Denmark was out of line with all the other small white rosebushes.

The Princess spent the rest of the afternoon searching carefully through garden after garden. A viburnum was also not quite where it should be. The same thing was true of a white lilac in the Grand Parterre, and a lemon tree in a big round wooden tub in the Carrefour de la Reine. So many deviations could hardly be put down to accident; one of the gardeners was deliberately creating disorder. It was her duty to report this to her father, who would straightway have the wicked gardener, and perhaps all the other gardeners, beheaded. But he would also have the white rosebush and the viburnum and the lilac and the lemon tree moved back to where they belonged, and this she was not sure she wanted to have happen. It stands to reason, the Princess said to herself, that the guilty person must work after dark, for to spread disorder through the palace gardens in broad daylight would be far too dangerous.

That night, instead of dancing all the figures of a cotillion, she sent her partner for an ice and slipped unnoticed through one of the ballroom windows. There was a full moon. The gardens were entrancing, and at this hour not open to the public. Walking through a topiary arch, the Princess came upon a gardener's boy in the very act of transplanting a snowball bush. Instead of calling out for the palace guards, she stood measuring with her eyes by exactly how much this particular snowball bush in its new position was out of line with the other snowball bushes.

The gardener's boy got up from his knees and knocked the dirt off his spade. "The deviation is no more than exists between the North Pole and the North Magnetic Pole," he said, "but it serves to restore the balance of Nature." And then softly, so softly that she barely heard him, "I did not know there was anyone like you."

"Didn't you?" the Princess said, and turned to look at him. After a moment she turned away. For once she found it not easy to be gracious, simple, and direct. She said—not rudely, but as she would have to a friend if she had had one—"I have the greatest difficulty in managing to be alone for five minutes."

"I don't wonder," he said. Their eyes met, full of inquiry. "When I look at you, I feel like sighing," he said. "My mouth is dry and there is a strange weakness in my legs. I don't remember ever feeling like this before."

"I know that when Papa and Mama and Aunt Royal and the others come out on the balcony and bow to the cheering multitudes, I ought to be there with them, and that I embarrass Papa by my absence, but I do not feel that appearing in public from time to time is enough. There are other things that a ruling family could do. For example, one could learn to play some musical instrument—the cello, or the contrabassoon. Or get to know every single person in the kingdom, and if they are in trouble help them."

"Your every move and gesture is sudden and free, like the orioles," the gardener's boy said.

"Also, I am very tired of wearing the same emeralds to the same operas year after year," the Princess said. "Isn't it nice about the birds. One says 'as the crow flies,' meaning in a straight line, but when you stand and watch them, it turns out that they often fly in big circles."

"If I had known I would find you here," the gardener's boy said, "I would have come straight here in the first place."

"Or they fly every which way," the Princess said. "And nothing can be done about it."

"I cannot tell you," the gardener's boy said, "how I regret the year I spent wandering through China, and the six months I spent in the Caucasus, and those two years in Persia, and that four months and seventeen days in Baluchistan."

By this time they were sitting on an antique marble bench some distance away. They could hear the music of violins, and the slightest stirring of the air brought with it the perfume of white lilacs.

"What made you take up gardening?" the Princess asked. "One can see at a glance that you are of royal blood. Was it to get away from people?"

"No, it was not that, really. At my father's court it is impossible to get away from people. There is no court calendar and no time of the day or night that anybody is supposed to be anywhere in particular, and so they are everywhere. I long ago gave up trying to get away from them."

"How sad!"

"Until I set off on my travels, I didn't know the meaning of solitude. In my country it is the fashion to admire any form of deviation. The streets of the capital start out impressively in one direction and then suddenly swerve off in quite another, or come to an end when you least expect it. To go straight from one engagement to another is considered impolite. It is also not possible. In school, children aren't taught how to add and subtract, but, instead, the basic principles of numerology. As you can imagine, the fiscal arrangements are extraordinary. People do not attempt to balance their checkbooks, and neither does the bank. No tree or bush is ever pruned, and the public gardens are a jungle where it is out of the question for a human being to walk, though I believe wild animals like it.

About a decade ago, the musicians decided that the interval between, say, C and C sharp didn't always have to be a half tone—that sometimes it could be a whole tone and sometimes a whole octave. So there is no longer any music, though there are many interesting experiments with sound. The police do not bother men who like to dress up in women's clothing and vice versa, and the birth rate is declining. In a country where no thought is ever carried to its logical conclusion and everybody maunders, my father is noted for the discursiveness of his public statements. Even in private he cannot make a simple remark. It always turns out to be a remark within a remark that has already interrupted an observation that was itself of a parenthetical nature. As it happens, I am a throwback to a previous generation and a thorn in the flesh of everybody."

"How nice that there is someone you take after," the Princess murmured. "I am said to resemble no one."

"As a baby I cried when I was hungry," the Prince said, caught up in the pleasure of talking about himself, "and sucked my thumb in preference to a jewelled pacifier. Applying myself to my studies, I got through my schooling in one third the time it took my carefully selected classmates to finish their education, and this did not make me popular on the playing field. Also I was neat in my appearance, and naturally quick, and taciturn—and this was felt as being in some oblique way directed against my father. From his reading of history he decided that the only way to make a troublesome crown prince happy was to abdicate in his favor, and he actually started to do this. But the offer was set in a larger framework of noble thoughts and fatherly admonitions, some of which did perhaps have an indirect bearing on the situation, if one could only have sorted them out from the rest, which had no bearing whatever and took him farther and farther afield, so that he lost sight of his original intention, and when we all sat down to dinner the crown was still on his head . . . I have never talked to anyone the way I am talking to you now. Are you cold sitting here in the moonlight? You look like a marble statue, but I don't want you to become chilled."

She was not cold, but she got up and walked because he suggested it.

"Two days later," he continued, "I saddled my favorite Arabian horse and rode off alone to see the world. When I first came here, walking in a straight line through streets that were at right angles to each other, I felt I had found a second home. After a few weeks, as I got to know the country better—"

Seeing his hesitation, she said, "You do not need to be tactful with me. Say it."

"My impressions are no doubt dulled from too much travelling," he began tactfully, "but it does seem to me that there are things that cannot be said except in a roundabout way. And things that cannot be done until you have first done something else. A wide avenue that you can see from one end to the other is a splendid sight, but when every street is like this, the effect is of monotony." Then, with a smile that was quite dazzling with happiness, the Prince went on, "Would you like to know my name? I am called Arqué. Before setting off on the Grand Tour, I should have supplied myself with letters of introduction, but I was in too much of a hurry, and so here, as in the other countries I visited, I knew no one. I could not present myself at the palace on visiting day because I was travelling incognito. I was free to pack my bags and go, but I lingered, unable to make up my mind what country to visit next, and one morning as I was out walking, an idea occurred to me.

I hurried back to the inn and persuaded a stableboy to change clothes with me. Fifteen minutes later I was at the back door of the palace asking to speak to the head gardener. Shortly after that I was on my hands and knees, pulling weeds. The rest you know."

They were now standing beside a fountain. Looking deeply into her eyes, he said, "In my father's kingdom there is a bird called the nightingale that sings most beautifully."

"A generation ago there were still a few nightingales here," the Princess said, "but now there aren't any. It seems they do not like quite so much order. This is the first time I have ever walked in the gardens at night. I didn't know that this plashing water would be full of moonlight."

"Your eyes are full of moonlight also," the Prince said.

"I feel I can tell you anything," the Princess said.

"Tomorrow," Prince Arqué said, glancing in the direction of the rosebush that was named after the Queen of Denmark, "I will move them all back."

"Oh, no!" the Princess cried. "Oh, don't do that! They are perfect just the way they are."

"Would you like to be alone now?" the Prince inquired wistfully. "I cannot bear the thought of leaving you, but I know that you like to have some time to yourself."

"I cannot bear to leave you either," the Princess said.

SINCE they had both been brought up on fairy tales, they proposed to be married amid great rejoicing and live happily ever after, but the Minister of State had other plans, and did not favor an alliance with a country whose foreign policy was so lacking in straightforwardness.

The Princess Horizon was locked in her room, Prince Arqué was informed that his visa had expired, and they never saw each other again. According to the most interesting and least reliable of the historians of the period, Prince Arqué succeeded his father to the throne, and left the royal palace, which was as confusing as a rabbit warren, for a new one that he had designed himself and that set the fashion for straight lines and right angles in architecture. From architecture it spread to city-planning, and so on. King Arqué had a son who was terribly long-winded, and a thorn in his flesh.

As for the Princess Horizon, it seems she found a new and rather dreadful way of disappearing. From the day that she was told she could not marry Prince Arqué, she never smiled again, and no one knew what was on her mind or in her heart. When her sympathetic ladies-in-waiting had finished grouping themselves around her chair, to their dismay she was sitting in it. When the royal family appeared on a balcony that was reserved for moments of history, the Princess was with them and bowed graciously to the cheering multitudes. She opened bazaars, laid cornerstones, distributed medals, and went to the opera. When the exiled King of Poland asked for her hand in marriage, the offer was considered eminently suitable and accepted. The exiled King of Poland turned out to have a flaw in his character also, but of a more ordinary kind; he had a passion for gambling. Ace of hearts, faro, baccarat, hazard, roulette—he played them all feverishly, and feverishly the courtiers imitated him, mortgaging their castles and laying waste their patrimony so they could go on gambling. The trees in their neglected orchards soon took on a more natural shape, and sorrowing elders grew bent with age. The common people aped the nobility as usual. New roads were carelessly built and therefore less straight than the old ones, the law of the land became full of loopholes, and only now and then did someone indulge in straightforward, logical thinking.

18

The woman who had no eye for small details

ONCE upon a time there was a woman who had no
eye for those small details and dainty effects that
most women love to spend their time on—curtains and
doilies, and the chairs arranged so, and the rugs so, and
a small picture here, and a large mirror there. She did
not bother with all this because, in the first place, she
lived alone and had no one but herself to please, and,
anyway, she was not interested in material objects. So her
house was rather bare, and, to tell the truth, not very comfortable. She lived very much in her mind, which fed upon
books: upon what Erasmus and Darwin and Gautama
Buddha and Pascal and Spinoza and Nietzsche and St.
Thomas Aquinas had thought; and what she herself
thought about what they thought. She was not a homely
woman. She had good bones and beautiful heavy hair,
which was very long, and which she wore in a braided
crown around her head. But no man had ever courted her,
and at her present age she did not expect this to happen. If
some man had looked at her with interest, she would not

have noticed it, and this would, of course, have been enough to discourage further attentions.

Her house was the last house on a narrow dirt road, deep in the country, and if she heard the sound of a horse and buggy or a wagon, it was somebody coming to see her, which didn't often happen. She kept peculiar hours, and ate when she was hungry, and the mirror over the dressing table was sometimes shocked at her appearance, but since she almost never looked in it, she was not aware of the wisps of hair that needed pinning up, the eyes clouded by absent-mindedness, the sweater with a button missing, worn over a dress that belonged in the rag bag. A blind man put down in her cottage would have thought there were two people, not one, living in it, for she talked to herself a great deal.

Birds in great numbers nested in the holes of her apple trees and in the ivy that covered her stone chimney. Their cheeping, chirping sounds were the background of all that went on in her mind. Often she caught sight of them just as they were disappearing, and was not sure whether she had seen a bird or only seen its flight—so like the way certain thoughts again and again escaped her just as she reached out for them. When the ground was covered with snow, the birds closed in around the house and were at the feeding stations all day long. Even the big birds came—the lovely gentle mourning doves, and the pheasants out of the woods, and partridge, and quail. In bitter weather, when the wind was like iron, she put pans of warm water out for them, and, in a corner sheltered from the wind, kept a patch of ground swept bare, since they wouldn't use the feeders. And at times she was as occupied—or so she told herself—as if she were bringing up a large family of children, like her sister.

Her sister's children were as lively as the birds, and even noisier, and they were a great pleasure to the woman who lived all alone, when she went to visit them. She played cards with them, and let them read to her, and listened to all that they had to say, which their mother was too busy to do. While she was there she was utterly at their disposal, so they loved her, and didn't notice the wisps of hair that needed pinning up, or that there was a button missing from her sweater, or the fact that her dress was ready for the rag bag. Looking around, she thought how, though her sister's house was small and the furniture shabby, everything her eye fell upon was there because it served some purpose or because somebody loved it. The pillows were just right against your back, the colors cheerful, the general effect of crowdedness reflected the busy life of the family. Their house was them, in a way hers was not. Her house, to be her, would have had to be made of pine boughs or have been high up in some cliff. The actual house sheltered her and that was all that could be said for it.

Her nieces and nephews would have been happy to have her stay with them forever, but she always said, "I have to get back to my little house," in a tone of voice grownups use when they don't intend to discuss something.

"Your house won't run off," her sister would say. "Why do you worry about it so? I don't see why you don't make us a real visit."

"Another time," the woman said, and went on putting her clothes in her suitcase. The real reason that she could not stay longer she did not tell them, because she knew they would not take it seriously: she could not bear the thought of the birds coming to the feeders and finding nothing but dust and chaff where they were accustomed to find food. So home she went, promising to come back soon, and never outstaying her welcome.

B UT no woman—no man, either—is allowed to live completely in her mind, or in books, or with only the birds for company. One day when she opened her mailbox, which was with a cluster of other mailboxes at a crossroads a quarter of a mile away, there was a letter from her sister. She put it in her pocket, thinking that she knew what was in it. Her sister's letters were, as a rule, complaining. Her life was hard. Her handsome, easygoing, no-good husband had deserted her, and she supported herself and the children by fine sewing. She worried about the children, because they were growing up without a father. And though they were not perfect, their faults loomed larger in her eyes than they perhaps needed to. In any case, she was tired and overworked and had no one else to complain to.

Hours later, the woman remembered that she had not read the letter, which turned out to be only three lines long: "I am very sick and the doctor says I must go to the hospital and there is no one to look after the children. Please come as soon as you can get here."

All the time the woman was packing, she kept thinking now about her poor sister and now about the poor birds. For it was the middle of the winter, there was deep snow on the ground, and the wind crept even into the house through the crack under the door, through closed windows. She filled the feeders to overflowing with seeds and suet, and sprinkled cracked corn on the ground, knowing that in two days' time it would all be gone. It was snowing again when she locked the door behind her and started off, with her old suitcase, to the nearest farmhouse. She would have to ask the farmer to hitch up his horse and sleigh and drive her to the station in the village, where she could take a train to the place where her sister lived.

Fluffed out with cold, the birds sat and watched her go.

When she came back she was not alone. The farmer's sleigh was full of children with sober, pale faces. They climbed down without a word and stood looking at their new home. The woman had left at the beginning of February, and it was now nearly the end of March. The snow on the roof, melting, had made heavy cornices of ice along the eaves, and the ice, melting, had made long, thin icicles. The woman got down, and thanked the farmer, and stood looking around, to see if there were any birds. The trees were empty, there was no sound in the ivy, and the cold wind went right through her.

"Come, children," she said, as she searched through her purse for her door key. "Let us go in out of the cold. You can help me build a fire."

Inside it seemed even colder, but the stoves soon made a difference. She was so busy feeding the children and warming their beds that she scarcely had time to go to the door and throw out a handful of seed on the snow. No birds came. The next day, she swept a bare place in the sheltered corner, and put out corn for the pheasants and quail, and filled the feeders. But she did all this with a heavy heart, knowing that it was to no purpose. And her sister's death had been a great tragedy and she did not see how she could fill her sister's place in the children's hearts or do for them what their mother had done. The corn on the ground, the sunflower seeds in the feeders were untouched when night fell.

Inside the house there was the same unnatural quiet. The woman did not talk to herself, because she was not alone. The children said, "Yes, please," and "No, thank you," and politely looked at the books she gave them to read, and helped set the table, and brought in wood and water, but

she could see that they were waiting for only one thing—
to go home. And there was no home for them to go to now
but here. They did not quarrel with one another, as they
used to, or ask her riddles, or beg her to play Old Maid
with them. In the face of disaster they were patient. They
could have walked on air and passed through solid walls.
They looked as if they could read her mind, but theirs
were no longer open to her. Though they cried at home,
they did not cry here—at least not where she could see
them. In their beds in the night, she had no doubt.

THE next morning, exhausted, she overslept, and when
she came into the kitchen the children were crowded at
the window. Something outside occupied their attention so
they could hardly answer when she said good morning to
them.

"Your birds have come back," the oldest nephew said.

"Oh surely not!" she cried, and hurried to the window.
On the ground outside, in the midst of all the whiteness and
brightness, it was like a party. The cardinals, the chicka-
dees, the sparrows, the juncos, the nuthatches, the jays
were waiting their turn at the feeders, pecking at the corn
in the sheltered place, leaving hieroglyphs in the snow.
Somehow, mysteriously, deep in the woods perhaps, they
had managed without her help. They had survived. And
were chirping and cheeping.

"We got our own breakfast," the children said. Though
they didn't yet know it, they would survive also.

The tears began to flow down her cheeks, and the children came and put their arms around her. "So silly of me,"
she said, wiping her eyes with her handkerchief, only to
have to do it again. "I thought they were all—I didn't think

they'd survive the cold, with nobody to feed them, for so long." Then more tears, which kept her from going on. When she could speak, she said, "I know it's not—I know you're not happy here the way you were at home." She waited until she could speak more evenly. "The house is not very comfortable, I know. I'm different from your mother. But I loved her, and if you will let me, I will look after you the best I can. We'll look after each other."

Their faces did not change. She was not even sure that they heard what she had said. Or if they heard but didn't understand it. Together, they carried warm water in pans, they swept off a new place for the quail, they hung suet in bags from the branches of the hemlock. They got out the bird book, and from that they moved on to other tasks, and the house was never quite so sad again. Little by little it changed. It took on the look of that other house, where everywhere about you there were traces of what someone was doing, as sharp and clear and interesting as the footprints of the birds in the snow.

19

The woodcutter

O NCE upon a time there was an old woodcutter who
lived in a hut in a clearing in the forest, far from
any town. Behind the hut there was a pond with carp
in it, and in the forest there were wild apple trees and
blackberry brambles and rabbits and deer. With all this
to draw upon, the woodcutter and his wife lived well
enough until, on the doorstep of their old age, a young
King, hunting in the forest, became separated from his
court and rode up to the hut and saw the pond and the
circle of tall pine trees around the clearing and said to
himself, "Here if anywhere I shall find the meaning of
life."

He got down off his horse and knocked on the door of
the hut and explained to the old woman that he was lost.

"Now, isn't that a pity," the old woman said. "Come in
out of the cold and warm yourself. I have lived so long in
this hut that I don't remember any more how to get out of
the forest, but my husband is cutting wood and when he
comes home for his supper he will show you the way."

She was embarrassed to find herself alone in the company of the King, and so while he was warming himself at

the fire she took an apple out to his horse, waiting patiently beside the door of the hut. When she came inside she asked, "Aren't you afraid to leave your fine horse without even tying the reins to a sapling?"

"No," said the young King, "the horse is well trained. He will not run away, and if he did, it would not matter. I have other horses."

He began to talk to the old woman about the subject that was dearest to his heart—the meaning of life—but she didn't understand a word he said. She saw that the King was sitting too near the fire, and the smell of burning wool was so strong in her nostrils that at last she had to speak to him about it.

"Hadn't you better move away from the fire? Your fine cloak is being scorched and that would be a pity."

"No," the King said, "I like the warmth. The castle I am living in at the moment is on a hill and often cold and drafty. If the cloak is scorched it does not matter. I have other cloaks."

The old woman glanced at the wooden peg by the door where her husband's old cloak of rough homespun hung when he was at home. In the room there was no sound but the crackling of the fire, and the King, glancing around, said, "Aren't you ever lonely here?"

"No," said the old woman. "My husband comes home at nightfall, and I know that I have to get his supper for him, and therefore I am never lonely."

"But what if something happened to your husband?" the young King asked.

"Nothing could happen to my husband that wouldn't also happen to me," the old woman said. "I am not afraid."

"In the castle I am now living in," the King said, "there are many people, all of them ready and anxious to wait upon me and be near me. If one of them gets sick and dies, there are always others ready and anxious to take his place."

The old woman noticed the wrinkles in the young King's forehead and the pallor of his face.

"You are not married?" she asked.

"No," the King said.

"That is a pity," she said, shaking her head.

"No," the King said, "it doesn't matter. If I could have two queens, I would have married long ago, but the archbishop will not permit me to have two queens, and I do not wish to be dependent on any one person, and therefore I have never married."

Just at dark the woodcutter came into the cottage, and when the two men stood side by side, the old woman saw that the King, in spite of his crown, was not as tall as her husband nor as broad in the shoulder.

The three of them sat down to supper, and afterward the woodcutter lit his lantern and the King leapt on his horse and they went off through the forest. As soon as they were out of sight of the hut, the King began to speak to the old woodcutter about the meaning of life. The woodcutter listened respectfully, and when the King had finished he waited for the woodcutter's reply, for he was genuinely concerned about the welfare of his subjects and liked to hear their views on matters of importance. But instead of answering him, the woodcutter raised his arm and pointed. There in the distance the King saw the lights of the castle.

EARLY the next morning, the forest rang with the sound of marching feet, the trample of ox teams, and the creak of cart wheels. A thousand workmen surrounded the hut in the forest. They had brought their tools with them, and they began to dig a deep ditch around the wood-cutter's hut and to widen the forest paths for roads. When the old woman came out of the hut and remonstrated with them, the workmen shrugged their shoulders.

"It is the King's will," they said.

"But why does he have to dig his ditch here?" the old woman asked.

"It is for a moat," the workmen said.

"But what good is a moat where there is no castle?"

"When we are finished there will be a castle where your hut now stands," the workmen said.

"But the King already has another castle," the old woman said, "and this poor hut is the only home we have under the sky."

"The King has many castles," the workmen said. "This castle is for him to come to when he needs solitude to consider the meaning of life."

Since she could get no better reason from them, the old woman threw a shawl over her head and ran off through the forest. By nightfall the moat was completed and the water from the pond let into it. The carp from the pond swam round and round the woodcutter's hut, and the rabbits and deer crossed and recrossed the new road that led out of the forest. It had taken the old woman all day to find her husband, and she was half crazed with calling and searching for him. When they saw their hut surrounded by a moat over which there was as yet no bridge, the wood-cutter could not speak for despair, but out of habit the old woman gathered sticks for a fire, and they got ready to pass the night with neither food nor shelter.

"At least the forest is still the same," she said. "We still have the stars in the sky," and she fell asleep with her head in her husband's lap. The woodcutter stayed awake to tend the fire, but he was worn out from his day's work and from grief at losing his home, and his head began to nod and the heat of the fire made him drowsier and drowsier.

At midnight a procession of horsemen and men carrying torches came into the forest and arrived at the clearing. The two figures beside the ashes of their fire did not stir, and the King, dismounting from his horse, thought for a moment that they were statues brought by the workmen for his new castle. Then he realized his mistake and shook the woodcutter, but there was no response. The woodcutter had gone where no king's touch would waken him, and what had happened to the woodcutter also happened to his wife. In anger the King turned to the court chamberlain and asked, "Why didn't the men build a bridge so that the two old people, who, after all, were kind to me, could get to their hut?"

The court chamberlain hemmed and hawed and said, "The royal order was to build a moat. Nothing was said about a bridge over the moat."

"No," the King said thoughtfully. And then, "It doesn't matter. I have other woodcutters. Tell them to come and cut wood in this forest. If I don't hear the sound of the axe ringing in the distance I will be lonely here."

But it turned out, strangely, that there were no more woodcutters. All the firewood in the kingdom was cut by the old man who now sat with his chin resting on his breast, his gray hair whitened by new-fallen snow.

The King stood and looked at him a long time, while the torches burned down and the courtiers shivered with the cold and waited for their royal master to be of one mind or another. At daybreak he turned to them and said, "I have found the meaning of life."

They stood waiting for him to announce that life is good or that life is bad, but instead he took off his crown and handed it to the court chamberlain.

"From now on I will be the woodcutter," he said, "and live in this hut."

"But you are our king," the court chamberlain said.

"No," the King said. "And in any case it doesn't matter. There are many kings and many people ready and anxious to be kings. I am the only one who is ready and anxious to take the place of this poor woodcutter."

Bearing the crown carefully in his left hand, the court chamberlain mounted his horse and rode back into the forest, and the courtiers, in the order of their rank and according to established precedence, mounted their horses and followed him.

20

The shepherd's wife

THERE was a shepherd's wife in Bohemia who was greatly
saddened when, after twelve years of being married,
she still had no children. Her husband was a quiet man,
large and slow-moving and dependable, and she loved him
with all her heart, but he had no gift for speech, perhaps
from spending so much time with animals, and instead of
the prattle of childish voices that she so longed to hear,
the woman was forced to be content with the ticking
of the clock and the sound of the teakettle on the crane,
the singing of wet wood on the hearth. Sometimes her
husband was gone for days at a time, and then the sound
of her own footsteps grew unbearably loud, and she
thought that if only her husband would come home, so she
could hear his heavy sigh when he sat down and warmed
himself before the fire, and the dog's tail thumping, she
wouldn't ask for more—not even the children that had
been denied her.

For every deprivation there is always some gift, and the
shepherd's wife was famous throughout the village for her
ability to make things grow. The windows of her cottage
were full of flowering plants all winter long, and when

other women had trouble with their house plants—the leaves turning yellow and dropping off and no new green coming, or red spider, or white fly, or mealy bug, or aphids—when their favorite plants were, in fact, almost ready to be thrown on the compost heap, they would bring them to the shepherd's wife and say "Can you do anything with this? It used to have masses of blooms and now look at it!" and the shepherd's wife would make a place for the sick plant on the window sill on the south side of the kitchen, where the sun poured in all day long through the thick, round glass. A month later she would wrap the plant up carefully against the cold and deliver it to its owner, in full leaf, with new buds forming all over it.

"What ever do you do to make things grow?" the other women asked her. "Do you water them very often, or just every other day, or what is your secret?"

"To make plants grow," the shepherd's wife always said, "you have to look at them every day. If you forget about them or neglect them, they die."

The other women, whose households were blessed with children, never remembered this advice or quite believed in it, and there was even a rumor (for it was a very small place, and no one living there escaped the breath of slander) that the shepherd's wife was a witch.

Actually, there was more to it than she could ever quite bring herself to tell them. After all, they had their little Josephs and Johns and Mary Catherines, and she had only her Christmas cactus, her climbing geraniums, her white rosebush in its big tub, and her pink oleander. So she kept her secret, which was that she not only looked at every plant every day but also talked to them, the way some lonely people talk to animals or to themselves.

"Now," she would say, standing in front of the Christmas cactus, when the shepherd was out of the house and there was nobody around to hear her, "I know you're slow by nature, but so is my husband, and he has his happy moments and you should have yours. All you need to do is grow a little." Then she would pass on to the pink oleander. "What is *this?*" she would exclaim. "Why are your leaves dry and stiff this morning? Too much sun? Very well, behind the curtain you go until you are feeling better." Then, to the white rosebush: "Just because those great geraniums are almost touching the ceiling and crowding everything else out, you needn't think I don't know you are here. Besides, if you will notice, the geranium blossom has no scent. . . ." So she talked to the plants, as if they were children, and, like children, they grew and grew and blossomed over and over again all winter long.

ONE day, the old midwife who always took care of the birth of children in the village came to the shepherd's wife and, drawing her to the chimney corner where the kettle was boiling for tea, said "It's time somebody told you—you are with child."

At first the woman wouldn't believe it, although the midwife had never been known to make a mistake in these matters, and when she did believe that it was true, she was still not happy. "I've waited too long," she told herself. "If children had come when I was younger, it would have been very different. Now I don't know what will happen to me. I may die. And if nothing dreadful happens to me, something will certainly happen to my Christmas cactus, my climbing geraniums, my rosebush, and my pink oleander as soon as I take to my bed and cannot look at them and talk to them the way they are used to."

She didn't confide these fears to her husband, not wanting to spoil his happiness, but he knew her moods, and when he saw that in spite of the blessing that had come to them she was still heavy-hearted, he stayed home with her more, and arranged with the other shepherds to mind his flocks for him. Wherever she went about the cottage, scrubbing and cleaning and putting things in order, he watched her, hoping to find out what was on her mind.

Having him around the house so much made her nervous, and when the plants began to drop their leaves and turn yellow because she couldn't bring herself to talk to them in front of anybody, she saw the fulfillment of her worst fears. She became pale, her shoulders drooped, she never spoke of the future, never discussed with her husband what they might name the child, or even whether it was going to be a boy or a girl. It was as if the child inside her were somebody else's plant that she could care for with her body but must not become attached to.

When her time came, the shepherd ran through the snowy night to the poor hovel that was all the midwife had for a roof over her head, and brought her hobbling back across the ice and snow. He put the kettle on the crane and built up a roaring fire and tried to stop his ears against the sounds that came from the bedroom—sounds that made his heart stop with terror. He felt a desperate need to talk to someone, but the midwife was too busy, coming and going with her hot cloths and her basins of boiling water, and she would not listen to him. At last he turned to the plants and told them his fears. Immediately before his eyes the limp leaves began to straighten, the stems to turn green. He went on talking to them without perceiving that anything unnatural had happened. His wife's secret was safe. He was a man, and so it didn't interest him.

In the terrible course of time, while the shepherd sat with his head in his hands and cursed the day he was born, the moans in the next room became screams and cries, and then suddenly there were two cries instead of one. A little while later, the midwife appeared with a baby, the smallest that had ever been seen in the village. She removed the soft woollen scarves it was wrapped in, and showed it to the shepherd, who sprang up with such pride in his heart and such happiness in his face that the newborn babe responded and began to wave its arms feebly.

"You have a daughter," the old midwife said.

"From God," the shepherd said.

"A very small, meachin, puny daughter," the old midwife said scornfully.

"She will be the most beautiful and proud woman that ever lived," the shepherd said. "She will be as beautiful and proud as the forests of Bohemia."

When the old midwife left him to care for the mother and child, he turned again to the plants on the window sill, and when the sun came up and lighted their leaves, he was still telling them about his newborn daughter.

D AY after day the plants grew, but the baby did not, and the mother remained feverish and pale on her bed and did not love her child. When the shepherd knelt beside her and asked how she was feeling, she shook her head and did not say what she thought, which was, I shall never get up out of this bed.

She didn't dare ask about the plants—if they had died one by one, and been thrown out—but one day, after the midwife had gone to assist at the birth of another child, and the man had left the house for a few minutes to

see about his sheep, the woman got up out of bed, intending to get back in again as soon as she had satisfied her
curiosity. She tottered into the kitchen expecting to see the
dry stalks of all her beloved plants, or maybe nothing at all,
and what met her eyes was a green bower of blossoms such
as she, who was famous throughout the village for her ability to make things grow, had never managed to have. The
scent of the flowers was heavy in the low-ceilinged room,
and as she stood there, looking at her Christmas cactus, her
climbing geraniums, her white rosebush, and her pink
oleander, the tight center of her heart opened, petal by
petal.

She ran into the bedroom, where the child fretted, and
brought it, cradle and all, into the room where the flowers
were. "This is my very own daughter," she said. "She's
very small, and she cries all the time, but some of you were
sickly too, at first, and dropped your leaves, and showed
every sign of not flourishing, and now look at you. Dearest
heart," she said, pulling back the woollen cover until she
could see the shadowy silken skin at the baby's throat.
"Now you must grow. You must stop fretting. You must
sleep," she said, unbuttoning her dress and helping the tiny
pale mouth to find her breast. "You must grow tall and
proud and beautiful, like the forests of Bohemia."

21

The man who loved to eat

ONCE upon a time there was a man who loved to eat. Two helpings of this, a little more of that, and when he was full, out of consideration for his wife's feelings, he had a little more of something else. Half an hour after he had got up from the table, he would pass through the kitchen and, seeing the remains of the roast on its platter, think regretfully, It won't be the same tomorrow. And then, after a guilty look over his shoulder, he would snitch a small piece of outside, not at all bothered by the fact that he was putting roast beef on top of prune whip. Oddly enough, it did not occur to him that he was greedy until this was pointed out to him at a dinner party by the woman who sat on his left and who, for one reason and another, did not enjoy seeing people eat. He thought a moment and then said, "Yes, it's true. I am greedy," and he decided to leave part of his dessert, but it was a particularly good strawberry mousse, and the next time he looked down, his plate was bare. He should have weighed three hundred pounds and waddled when he walked, but instead he was thin as a rail. He had always been thin. All that food did for him was keep up his appetite.

Though his wife ate sparingly, being mindful of her figure, she liked to cook for him, and his friends smiled as they watched him settle down to a menu. It is not moral perfection that most people find endearing but an agreeable mixture of strong points and frailties. His weakness was clearly the love of food, and he confidently expected to eat his way into his grave. But just when you think you know how things are going to be, it turns out that they aren't that way after all. "Will you have another helping of potatoes?" his wife asked one evening, and he started to say "Yes," as usual, and to his surprise he heard himself say "No." He had had enough. He couldn't eat any more, not even to please her. He wondered if he was coming down with something, and so, privately, did she.

The next morning he woke up feeling perfectly all right, and ate a huge breakfast, and that should have been the end of it, but there was a nagging doubt in the back of his mind: what happened once could happen again. He tried not to think about it. Four days later, when he sat down to the table, he found that once more he had no appetite. This time he was really frightened, and the nagging doubt moved from the back of his mind to the front, and stayed there. He ate, but out of the sense that it was something one must do. No real craving. At breakfast he did not find himself having just one more slice of buttered toast, with currant jelly on it because the other four slices had been either plain or with orange marmalade. He did not say, eying his wife's plate, "If that piece of bacon is going begging . . ." or "If you're not going to eat your English muffin. . . ." He—who was never melancholy—caught himself out in a sigh, and asked himself questions that are better left unasked.

When it came time for his annual checkup, his doctor

announced that his heart was normal and so was his blood pressure.

"You mean normal for my age," the man said gloomily.

"Yes. For a man of your age you're in very good shape. Appetite?"

"No appetite."

"Why not?"

"I don't know. I'm just not hungry. I'd just as soon never eat anything again as long as I live."

"We'll have to give you something for that," the doctor said, and he did. Though the man who loved to eat had absolute faith in any kind of medicine, and as a rule showed marked signs of improvement before the pills or the antibiotic could possibly have had a chance to take effect, this time it was different. The liver shots did nothing whatever for him.

About once every month or six weeks his appetite would return, for no reason, and he would stuff himself and think, Ah, now it is over. I can go on eating. . . . But the next time he sat down at the table, no sooner did he raise his fork to his mouth than with a look of utter misery he put it down again.

ONE day, passing by a secondhand bookstore, he happened to see, on a table of old, gritty, dehydrated books, the "Enchiridion" of Epictetus. He bought it and took it home and sat down to read it. "Require not things to happen as you wish, but wish them to happen as they do happen, and all will be well," Epictetus said, on page 8. The man who loved to eat took a pencil out of his inside coat pocket and underlined the sentence. A few pages farther on, he marked another: "Everything has two handles, the one by which it may be borne, the other by which it cannot." Suddenly he stopped reading and sat looking off into space. The expression on his face was that of a person who has just been saved from drowning. "Umm," he said, to nobody in particular. He read on a few more pages, and then, having absorbed all the Stoicism he could manage in one dose, he closed the book and went about his business, thankful that his pleasure in food lasted as long as it did—though what is thankfulness compared to a good appetite?

22

The epistolarian

Once upon a time there was an old maid who was the laughingstock of the hamlet she was born, raised, and died in. All she ever did was write letters. Other old maids taught school or took courses in typing and shorthand, put up twenty-seven quart jars of tomatoes, crocheted table mats, carried baskets to the poor, conducted a Saturday Morning Bible Class, devoted their lives to caring for invalid fathers, or joined in the general warfare of all women against disorder and dirt. But this old maid wrote letters, fifteen or twenty a day, over a period of many years, and not one of them, so far as the postmaster knew (and he was certainly in a position to know), was ever answered. She wrote to all her relatives, naturally, and no doubt her nieces and nephews would have answered the letters she sent them if once in a while a check had been enclosed, but this was not the case. The letters piled up on mantlepieces, on hall tables, and were not only unanswered but unread.

The bulk of the old maid's correspondence was directed to strangers—to the farmer whose cow had just given birth to a two-headed calf, to the leading actress of the day, to the most popular bishop, to the head of an anti-missionary society, or to a great scientist whose name was a household word, though his mathematical formulae were not widely understood. Sometimes the letters were addressed to shady characters as well—to the heartbreakingly handsome young housebreaker, to the model boy on trial for larceny and rape, to the blond young woman suing for a huge share in an old man's estate, to anybody, as a matter of fact, whose name, picture, and address appeared in the evening paper.

The editors of all the newspapers in the capital and in the chief provincial cities were supplied with long letters for their contributors' columns, and even though these letters, all in the same small indefatigable hand, were signed by various pseudonyms ("A Constant Reader," "An Observer," "One Who Hopes to See Justice Done") there were always far too many of them for the available space, and they accumulated, gathering dust on copy hooks and in the cubbyholes of the editors' roll-top desks. And at three minutes before noon each day the old maid hurried into the post office, her fingers stained with ink, her apron covered with ink blots, her hair untidy, her mind at peace as she thrust her morning's output through the wicket to be weighed, stamped, and disposed of in local and out-of-town bins. The people of the hamlet often gathered to count the fruit of her labor, and when there was an outsider present, somebody would make a circular sign with his forefinger, pointing at his temple. The stranger would grasp the significance of this gesture, nod, and smile. But it was always done behind the old maid's back, and not meant unkindly.

In time, the area covered by her letters increased until it took in all six continents (if you count Australia as a con-

tinent) and required such considerable daily sums for postage that the old maid was never able to afford new curtains
or a new dress, and it was feared she might even be going
without proper food. As proof of the contrary, it was
sometimes pointed out that the addresses were rising
rapidly in the social scale, and included countesses, dukes,
then a grand duke, a lord chief justice (who would certainly not let a poor woman starve that he knew anything
about), a lady-in-waiting, a court astrologer, a dowager
queen (at this point the villagers were sure there would be
trouble, that the police would come and take the poor silly
thing away and lock her up), and eventually a king and an
emperor.

The letters went on being mailed steadily and in quan-
tity, and then one day the old maid did not appear just
before noon, or after lunch; and that evening the post-
master kept open an hour after closing time, and finally
sent a boy to find out what was keeping her. Death was.
The boy knocked politely and, receiving no answer,
pushed open the door of her cottage and saw her lying on a
couch with her eyes closed, the nap she had lain down to
having proved to be a longer sleep than she had anticipated.
On her desk by the front window were the final letters,
thirty-eight in all, in their envelopes, addressed, sealed, and
ready for mailing. The boy gathered them up, tiptoed out
of the room, closed the door softly, and found the letters in
his coat pockets the next day.

THE funeral was brief and modest. The nephews and
nieces came and carried off the furniture, which was
not worth much, the best pieces having been sold to
provide postage for the letters that lay on their hall tables

and gathered dust on their mantelpieces. Only the post-master, passing the old maid's empty cottage with the "For Sale" sign on the door, felt that all had not been done for her that should have been done. Though she had never received any answers to the letters she spent her life writing, it was quite possible, he decided, that the people she wrote to would care about her, at least to the extent of wondering why the letters had stopped coming. So he took it upon himself to write a brief note to each of them, explaining that the village correspondent had passed on. Fortunately he was a methodical man and had kept a record of the names and addresses of everyone she wrote to, as a kind of curiosity and also to prove that an out-of-the-way part can be an important cog in the great machine. After he had reached the last name on the list and sealed the last envelope, an idea occurred to him. He steamed open the thousands of envelopes that lay in piles all over the post office, and to each of the thousands of notes he added a postscript, explaining that on such-an-such a day there would be a memorial service in honor of their friend.

He did not expect a living soul to attend, and he had difficulty persuading the assistant curate to prepare a short tribute for the occasion. But when the day came, the roads were blocked for miles around with all manner of carriages, many of them bearing coats of arms. Also farm wagons, delivery wagons, a dogcart, a gypsy wagon, and a hansom cab long out of use. Ten special trains had to be accommodated on the single siding. The village street was crammed with people who had come to the memorial service, and, the old maid's cottage being very cramped and small, the meeting was held out-of-doors. The curate's assistant, finding himself in the presence of a great multitude that included the highest dignitaries of state, aged members of the Academy of Arts and Sciences, the crowned heads of Europe and Asia, had stagefright and could not give his prepared speech, but there were many who did speak that day, extempore, from their place in the throng. The greatest living scientist, whose name was a household word, spoke of the old maid's letters—of what an inspiration they were to him, how intelligent and helpful her comment was, and how she had believed, long before the rest of the world, in his mathematical diagram of the five dimensions (length, breadth, thickness, time, and love). The greatest living poet praised her literary style (which was news to the village) and read a rather long poem in *terza rima*, the prologue to his unfinished epic, which he was dedicating to the old maid. The dowager queen said, with tears in her eyes, "So long as I heard from her, I knew I was remembered. Her letters gave me the courage to go on opening bazaars." The king said, "Through her letters I knew what my people were thinking, and that they were loyal to me. I always meant to write to her and never got around to it, more's the pity!" The emperor said, "Acting on her advice, I put off waging two very expensive wars. Every letter she wrote me is preserved in the Imperial Archives, bound in green vellum, for the use and admiration of a grateful posterity."

When the service was concluded, the criminal element, such as were on parole at the moment—second-story men, blackmailers, arsonists, dope peddlers, etc.—proceeded to the cemetery in a body and placed on the old maid's grave a floral tribute in the shape of a white quill pen made entirely of wired sweet peas. Attached to it was a florist's ribbon with the words "Yours very affy," in a raised silver-and-gold facsimile of her now famous handwriting.

23

The problem child

ONCE upon a time there was a man with a very beautiful and gentle wife, whose only thought was to
cherish and protect him, as his was for her, and their
happiness was completed by the birth of a daughter, who,
as she grew older, showed every sign of having inherited
her mother's beauty and loving nature. It was easy enough
to see what the future would bring, except that it did not
turn out that way. Suddenly, with no warning, the woman
took sick and died, and where then was the man's happiness
and the child's future?

For a time he was half mad with grief, and neglected his
affairs, and also neglected his child, though he didn't mean
to do this, and things steadily went from bad to worse, and
people shook their heads over the situation, and wished
there was something they could do. There was, and they
did it without realizing it. So many things were said in
praise of the dead woman's character that gradually, in the
man's mind, she changed, she became perfect, without a
flaw. All his memories of her, every affectionate and tender
thing she had ever said to him, fell away, and it was as if he

had been married to a photograph. One does not grieve forever over the loss of an ideal person. The man threw himself into his work, the color came back into his face, he smiled more often, and he was seen—dining in expensive restaurants, or in his car, headed for the country on a Saturday afternoon—with a pretty woman, a widow with two nearly grown daughters. No one blamed him for this, or had a word to say against her, except (and this was not really against her) that she wasn't exactly the person they would have expected him to show an interest in.

The wedding was small and quiet, and among the guests were a number of people who had been devoted to his first wife. He particularly wanted their approval and blessing on his marriage, and it was not withheld. But there was, of course, someone who was even more important to him. When the minister had pronounced them man and wife and they turned to face the wedding guests, the man's eyes sought out first of all his daughter. After his wife's death, in their bewilderment, they had clung to each other like drowning creatures, but during the last few weeks he had discovered that sorrow is more easily shared than happiness. Though she was docile about everything, he had no doubt but that in her heart she blamed him for not remaining faithful to her mother's memory. As he bent down and kissed her, he told himself that when she was a little older he would be able to put things in a light that she could understand and accept.

Unfortunately, children do not always want to understand, though sometimes, when one would prefer that they didn't, they understand all too well. The girl continued to reject her stepmother's affection, no matter how tactfully it was held out to her. Both the man and his wife had been prepared for this. What they did not expect was that it would go on so long. Since nothing was lacking to his happiness but his daughter's willingness to be a part of it, at times he could not help being exasperated with her. Up till now, she had never given him any trouble whatever, and so, as his wife pointed out, he was not used to being patient with her. When they were talking about the problem, late at night as they were undressing for bed, her conclusion always was that they should not add to the difficulty by exaggerating its seriousness. It would work itself out, with time. "Besides," she would say, as she sat at her dressing table putting cleansing cream on her face, "it isn't as if there was anything personal in the poor child's attitude. It's just a classical situation, and it has to be dealt with intelligently." Or she would say, "All that is perfectly true, and sometimes I feel like turning her over my knee and spanking her. But it doesn't help to get emotionally involved. Then you are fighting it out on her level, which is just what she wants."

When the man got home at night and his daughter threw her arms around him, he returned her embrace tenderly and kissed her on the cheek, and then after a second disengaged himself, for she was at an age when, the books all agreed, it was unwise to prolong demonstrations of affection. As one would have expected, the girl had no friends. She came straight home from school and went upstairs to her room and read until dinnertime. When the telephone rang it was always for her stepmother or her stepsisters. "Isn't there somebody you'd like to have come and spend the night with you?" the woman would ask, and the girl would shake her head and stare at her stepmother as if she were prying into something that was none of her business. "I know perfectly well I am exaggerating," the woman said afterward, as she and her husband were sitting together in their cosy little library, having their evening drink. "And in any case, I shouldn't let her get under my skin. It's just that it came on top of a long and rather difficult day. Let's not talk about it any more."

B UT they did talk about it, of course. It concerned them too deeply for them to be able to ignore—or forget about—what went on under their eyes every day. As she pointed out, it would have been far easier, when the girl did something she shouldn't have, to tell him and let him deal with it, but this was not really the way to break down her resistance. It was why so many women never succeeded in winning the affection of their stepchildren and were merely tolerated, when they were not actively disliked by them. Also the girl would know—how could she not know?—where the information came from.

She treated the girl exactly as she treated her own two daughters. If they had been disrespectful or disobedient, she would have had no choice but to punish them, for their own good. And since her stepdaughter was of an age when she could no longer be spanked, punishment had to take the form of withholding privileges and pleasures. So, when she was buying pretty new frocks for her own daughters, she chose something for her stepdaughter as well, and then, regretfully, put it back on the rack.

When the girl's behavior had been particularly flagrant, she was not allowed to eat with the family, and since it would not have done to have her confiding in the servants, she was made to eat in her room, from a tray. This was not a fairy tale, and so no fairy godmother appeared to change a pumpkin into a coach and all that, and send the girl off to a ball where the prince was waiting to fall in love with her. Instead, she cried herself to sleep, grew pale and thin, grew untidy in her appearance, and more and more obstinate in her conduct, and in every way possible confirmed her stepmother's view of the situation, which at times was close to despairing. They consulted an eminent child psychologist, who confirmed their fears and at the same time reassured them, for it was something of a comfort to know that the girl was like other emotionally disturbed children and not a unique case. He suggested that she would probably do better with a woman analyst. The therapist he recommended had studied with Anna Freud, and had a German accent, and was a chain smoker, and looked like a man, but she was very intelligent. The girl refused to play with the doll's house and the blocks, but she listened politely to what the woman said. In brief, what this amounted to was that the wicked stepmother of fairy tales is really a disguise—the child's repressed hostility toward its real mother, the rival for the affection of the father, becomes a projection. By forcing her stepmother into this role she had, in a sense, been keeping her dead mother alive and near her. The simple truth was that she did not hate her stepmother but was, if anything, too fond of her, and jealous of her stepsisters, who had a stronger claim on her stepmother's affection. Understanding this should have resulted in some change in the girl's behavior but it didn't. She kept the appointments with the analyst, though about other things she was very forgetful. But she answered all questions reluctantly and did not free associate. It appeared that she could not or would not believe that the analyst—that, indeed, anyone—was on her side. In the end, the analyst reported to her parents that there was no transference, and the treatments, which were, God knows, expensive enough, were discontinued.

Those overtures that were made to her—as a rule, privately—by old friends of the family, women who had known and loved her mother, the girl also rejected, or perhaps misunderstood, and so after one or two attempts the women stopped trying to do anything for her, in the belief that there was nothing they could do.

"What I fear," her stepmother said, "above everything else in this world, is that she will run off with the first man who looks at her. The Fuller Brush man, or somebody who works in a filling station." And that was exactly what happened, only it was a second-hand car salesman, and he was neither well made, nor well brought up, nor mentally her equal. He was not even very young.

A T first the girl's father was inclined to blame himself severely, and wanted to rush after the couple and make sure that they did not regret their action. But his wife convinced him that it was too soon for them to be anything but excited by what they had done, and he would simply be the villain who threatened their happiness. If it was the mistake that it appeared to be, then they must have time to realize it. If he made things too easy for them now, they would all the rest of their married life look to him to solve their problems. Reluctantly, he was prevailed upon to wait, to delay his forgiveness, to do nothing. And things did not turn out so badly as one might have supposed. Though the second-hand car salesman wasn't anything to write home about, the girl's only thought was to cherish and protect him, and for a time they were quite happy. When he took to drink and beat her, she left him and lived with someone else, for she had already experienced the worst that can happen to anybody, and knew that loving kindness can vanish overnight, and girls who lose their mother and are more handsome than their stepsisters have no one and therefore better learn to look after themselves.

24

The printing office

IN a certain large city, on a side street that was only
two blocks long, there was a two-story building with
a neon sign that read "R. H. Gilroy ♦ Printing." This
sign, which was strongly colored with orchid and blue
and flickered anxiously, was the crowning achievement of
thirty years of night work and staying open on Saturdays
and Sundays. R. H. Gilroy was a short, irascible man with
a green eyeshade, a pencil behind his ear, and a cigar butt
in the corner of his mouth. The sign didn't mention the
printer's wife, though it should have. She answered the
telephone and did the bookkeeping and wrote out bills
in a large, placid, motherly handwriting, and knew where
everything was and how to pacify her husband when he
got excited.

From her desk by the radiator, Maria Gilroy looked out
on the Apex Party Favors Company and A. & J. Kertock
Plumbing and Heating, directly across the street. She could
also see the upper stories of the Universal Moving and
Storage Company, two blocks north. At odd times of the
day, birds swooped down out of the air and settled on the
iron ladder that led from the roof of the storage company

to the cone-shaped roof of a water tank. The people of the neighborhood—boys lolling on the steps of the vocational high school, the policeman who stood under the marquee of Number 210 when it was raining, and others—took these birds to be pigeons. The printer's wife, who was born and brought up in Italy, knew they were not pigeons but doves. When her eyes demanded some relief from the strain of balancing figures that were, at the same time, too close to her face and too far from her heart, she would get up from her desk by the radiator, and go outdoors and stand looking up, shielding her eyes with her hand and straining for the sound that she remembered from her far-off childhood, and that she could sometimes almost hear, and might indeed have heard if a truck hadn't shifted into low gear or a bus hadn't backfired or if the children who lived over the Apex Party Favors Company and whose only place to play was the street had ever stopped yelling at each other. The silence that was always on the point of settling down on that not very busy street never actually did, and the birds circling through the silence of the upper air never settled on any perch lower than the iron ladder of the water tank of the Universal Moving and Storage Company.

The printer's wife tried various ways of coaxing them down. She bought a china dove in Woolworth's and set it in her window. She tried thought transference. She bought breadcrumbs at the delicatessen and scattered them on the sidewalk. But pigeons flying to and from the marble eaves of the post office saw the breadcrumbs and swooped down and strutted about on the sidewalk, picking and choosing and making sounds that were egotistical and monotonous, and of course they kept the doves away. When it rained, the breadcrumbs made a soggy mess on the sidewalk and the policeman left the shelter of the marquee and crossed the street and told the printer he was violating a city ordinance, which made him terribly excited. So she gave up trying to lure the birds closer and merely watched them. There was sometimes only one on the ladder, and there were never more than three. The business was open on Christmas Day, as usual, and on New Year's, and the birds were either on the ladder or in the air above it, but on the second of January she didn't see them all day, and when they weren't there the next morning, she said, "I wonder if something has happened to my birds."

The printer, who was reading proof for the sixth edition of a third-rate dictionary, bit into his damp, defeated cigar and reached for the pencil behind his ear. "Eeyah!" he exclaimed bitterly, and restored a missing cedilla. On the margin of the proof he wrote a sarcastic note for the typesetter, who was quick as lightning but not, unfortunately, a perfectionist. The printer's wife glanced over her shoulder and saw that the page he was correcting began with the word "doubt" and ended with "downfall." Her eyes traveled down the column of type until they stopped at "dove (duv)." In mounting excitement—for it must be a sign, it couldn't be just an accident—she read on hastily, through the derivation [ME. *douve*, akin to OS. *dūba*, D. *duif*, OHG. *tùba*, G. *taube*, ON. *dūfa*, Sw. *dufva*, Dan. *due*, Goth. *dūbo*, and prob. to OIr. *dub* black. See DEAF] and the first and second meanings, and arrived at the third. The words "emblem of the Holy Spirit" flickered on the page, though the harsh white fluorescent light did not alter, and she felt a moment of fright. Turning her eyes to the window, she saw the orchid faces of A. and J. Kertock, who had just padlocked the door of their shop and were about to go home to their dinner, content and happy with

((150))

using brass fitting when solid copper was specified and the thousand and one opportunities for padding a plumbing and heating bill. She nodded, and they—quite ready to admit that it takes all kinds to make a world and even though honesty is not the best policy there was no reason why the printer and his wife shouldn't pursue it if it gave them any pleasure—nodded in return. She wanted to throw open the window and ask them if they had seen the doves, but it wasn't that kind of a window.

The next morning, while she was tearing January 3 off her desk calendar, the doves settled down on their perch. It was a very cold day, and she was concerned for them. If they only had a little house they could go into, out of the wind, she kept thinking, and she was tempted to pick up the phone and call the Universal Moving and Storage Company. By the next morning, the wind had dropped and the air was milder, and that evening orchid and blue snow drifted gently down on the sidewalk and on the stone window-ledge, and on the tarred rooftops across the street. By eleven o'clock, when the neon sign was turned off, the street was like a stage setting.

AT noon on the sixth of January, the printer's wife put on her coat and her plastic boots and trudged through the snow to the delicatessen and came back with three chicken sandwiches on white, three dill pickles, and a paper container of cranberries. Leaning against the garbage cans of Number 210, where it certainly hadn't been a few minutes before, was a Christmas tree with some of the tinsel still on it. It had seen better days, but even so, in a landscape made up entirely of brick, stone, concrete, and plate glass, it was a pleasure to look at, and all afternoon the printer's wife kept getting up from her chair and glancing up the street to see if the tree was still there. At four o'clock she put on her coat and her plastic boots and went out into the street. The policeman saw her pick up the Christmas tree and carry it into the fishmarket, but he took no notice. When she walked into the printing shop a few minutes later with her arms full of green branches which the fishman had kindly chopped off for her, the printer saw her and didn't see her. Words and printer's symbols were the only things he ever saw and saw. She took the container of cranberries from the top drawer of the filing cabinet and then picked up the branches and went to the back of the shop and climbed the stairway to the second floor, where the back files and the office supplies were kept and where there was an iron stairs leading to a trapdoor that opened onto the roof. The roof of R. H. Gilroy ♦ Printing was flat and tarred, and it had a false front with an ornamental coping. In a corner where the wind would not reach it, the printer's wife made a shelter and sprinkled crumbs (she had eaten the slice of chicken but not the bread) and cranberries in among the green, forest-smelling boughs. The wind whipped at her coat, but she did not feel the cold. And all around her the rooftops were unfamiliar because of the snow, with here a pavilion and there an archway or a garden house or a grotto. The falling snow softened the sound of the trucks in the street, and the children who lived over the Apex Party Favors Company were indoors at that moment, playing under their Christmas tree, which sometimes stayed up until Easter, and was decorated with soiled paper hats, serpentines, crackers without any fortune in them, and papier-mâché champagne bottles. The street grew quieter and quieter and quieter and quieter, and at last, out of a sky as soft and as silent as the snow, three doves descended. They alighted on the ornamental coping and from the ornamental coping they flew to the chimney pots, and from there straight into the corner where the pine boughs had been prepared for them.

Aware that his wife had been standing behind his chair for some time, the printer looked up impatiently. Something in her face, an expression that he recognized as related in some remote way to printer's signs and symbols, made him take off his green eyeshade and place his cigar stub on the edge of the desk and follow her. As they passed the typesetter, she motioned to him, and he stopped his frantic machine and came too. At the top of the iron stair she turned and warned them not to speak. Then she pushed the trap door open slowly. The silence that had been coming and coming had arrived while she was downstairs, and as the two men stepped out onto the roof, bareheaded and surprised by the snow alighting on their faces, they heard first the silence and then the sound that came from the pine boughs.

"*Zenadoura macroura carolinensis*, the mourning dove," the printer whispered, quoting from the great unabridged dictionary that it was his life's dream to set up in type and print. His inkstained, highly-skilled, nervous hand sought and found his wife's soft hand. The typesetter crossed himself. The doves, aware of their presence but not frightened by it, moved among the boughs, seeking out the breadcrumbs, and with a slight movement of their feathered throats making sounds softer than snow, making signs and symbols of sounds, softer and more caressing than lŭv and dŭv, kinder than good, deeper than pēs.

25

The lamplighter

JUST before dark, when it was already dark inside the cottages and barns and outbuildings, the lamplighter came riding up one street and down the next, on his bicycle, with his igniting rod. He did not answer when people called a greeting to him, and so, long ago, they had stopped doing this—not, however, out of any feeling of unfriendliness. "There goes the lamplighter," they said, in exactly the same tone of voice that they said, "Why, there's the moon." Through the dusk he went, leaving a trail of lighted lamps behind him. And as if he had given them the idea, one by one the houses began to show a light in the kitchen, or the parlor, or upstairs in some low-ceilinged bedroom. Men coming home from the fields with their team and their dog, children coming home from their play, were so used to the sight of the lamplighter's bicycle spinning off into the dusk that it never occurred to them to wonder how the lamps he was now lighting got put out.

No two mornings are ever quite the same. Some are cold and dark and rainy, and some—a great many, in fact—are like the beginning of the world. First the idea of morning comes, and then, though it is still utterly dark and you can't see your hand in front of your face, a rooster crows, and you'd swear it was a mistake, because it is another twenty minutes before the first light, when the rooster crows again and again, and soon after that the birds begin, praising the feathered god who made them. With their whole hearts, every single bird in creation. And then comes the grand climax. The sky turns red, and the great fiery ball comes up over the eastern horizon. After which there is a coda. The birds repeat their praise, one bird at a time, and the rooster gives one last, thoughtful crow, and the beginning of things comes to an end. While all this was happening, the villagers were fast asleep in their beds, but the lamplighter was hurrying along on his bicycle, and when he came to a lamp, he would reach up with his rod and put it out.

The lamplighter was not young, and he lived all alone, in a small cottage at the far end of the village, and cooked his own meals, and swept his own floor, and made his own bed, and had a little vegetable garden and a grape arbor but no dog or cat for company, and the rooster that wakened him every morning before daybreak belonged to somebody else. It was an orderly, regular life that varied only in that everything the lamplighter did he did a few minutes earlier or a few minutes later than the day before, depending on whether the sky was clear or cloudy, and whether the sun was approaching the summer or the winter solstice. And since at dusk he was in too great a hurry to stop and speak to anyone, and in the morning there was never anyone to speak to, he lived almost entirely inside his own mind. There, over and over again, he relived the happiness that would never come again, or corrected some mistake that made his face wince with shame as he reached up with his rod and snuffed out one more lamp. The dead came back to life, just so he could tell them what he had failed to tell them when they were alive. Sometimes he married, and the house at the edge of the village rang with the sound of children's excited voices, and in the evening friends whose faces he could almost but not quite see came and sat with him under the grape arbor.

The comings and goings of his neighbors were never as real to him as his own thoughts, and so the first time he saw the woman in the long gray cloak walking along the path that went through the water meadows, at an hour when nobody was ever abroad, it was as if an idea had crossed his mind. She was a good distance away, walking with her back to him, and then the rising sun came between them and he couldn't see her any more, though he continued to peer over his shoulder in the direction in which he had last seen her.

He told himself that he needn't expect to see her ever again, because he knew every woman in the village and they none of them wore a long gray cloak, so it must be a stranger who had happened to pass this way, very early one morning, on some errand. He looked for her, even so, and the next time he saw her it was from such a great distance that he was not even sure it was the same person, but the beating of his heart told him that it was the woman he had seen crossing the water meadow. After that, he continued to see her—not often, and never at regular intervals, but always at some moment when he was not reliving the happiness that would never come again, or undoing old mistakes, or placating the dead, or peopling his solitary life with phantoms. Only when he wasn't thinking at all would he suddenly see her, and he realized that the distance between them was steadily diminishing. One morning he thought he saw her beckon to him, and he was so startled that he almost fell off his bicycle. He wanted to ride after her and overtake her, but something stopped him. What stopped him was the thought that he might have imagined it. While he was standing there debating what he ought to do and trying to decide whether she really had raised her arm and beckoned to him, suddenly she was no longer there. The early morning mists had hidden her. And in that moment his mind was made up.

Morning after morning, he peered into the distance and saw, through the mist, the familiar shape of a thatch-roofed cottage or a cow standing in a field, or a pollarded willow that had been there ever since he was a small boy. Or he saw a screen of poplars and the glint of water in the ditch that ran in a straight line through the meadows. But not what he was looking for. And as dusk came on and he got out his bicycle and his rod, there was a look of purpose on his face. If anybody had spoken to him as he rode past, stopping only when he came to a lamp that needed lighting, he would not have heard them.

And who said incontrovertibly that things are what they seem? that there is only this one life and no little door that you can step through into—into something altogether different.

One beautiful evening, when the warmth of the summer day lingered long past the going down of the sun, and the women stayed outside past their usual time, talking and not wanting to interrupt their conversation or the children's games, and one kind of half-light succeeded another, and the men came home from the fields and sat down to a glass of cold beer, and the dogs frolicked together, and finally there wasn't any more light in the sky, and in fact you could hardly see your hand in front of your face, suddenly a babble of voices arose all over the village, all saying the same thing: "Where is the lamplighter?"

People groped their way into their houses, muttering, "I don't understand it. This sort of thing has never happened before," and in one house after another a light came on, but the streets remained as dark as pitch. "If this happens again, we'll have to get somebody else to light the lamps," the village fathers said, standing about in groups, each with a lanthorn in his hand, and then, chattering indignantly among themselves, they set off in a body for the lamplighter's cottage, intending to have it out with him. A lot of good it did them.

26

The old man who was afraid of falling

ONCE upon a time there was an old man who was
afraid of falling. He put handrails on both sides of
the stairs and raised the turf to the level of his doorsill.
He also had bars put across the lower half of the windows
and the well covered over so he couldn't fall into it. At
considerable expense he had a railing built all around the
roof of his house so that if he should ever have to go
up and clean the gutters he could not fall off. And gradually he stopped going to the village to see his friends
because they lived in houses that had steps in unexpected
places and were foolishly indifferent to the risk they took
or the danger that awaited other people who came to their
houses.

Rather than walk down the steep path to the village, the
old man stayed at home and got his food from the farmers
driving by with carcasses of lamb and young pig, or their
carts piled high with vegetables. He was careful not to
climb up on the back of the cart, but made the farmers
drop the reins and get him what he wanted, since, as he
explained to them each time, he was afraid of falling. As

year after year went by, he stayed more and more in the house, letting his garden grow up in weeds, and making the farmers come to the door with their produce. When he went outside, something was always falling—in winter the snow, in spring the rain, in summer the flower petals, and in autumn the leaves, and it was more than he could bear to see this perpetual tragedy going on around him. In the end he drew the curtains and never looked on the outside world if he could help it.

Even indoors he was not altogether safe. A picture fell from the wall for no reason, or the cat jumped up on the table and he closed his eyes and waited for the crash that followed. He picked up the broken china and got rid of the cat. He took down all the pictures. And after that he felt as safe as anyone can feel in a world where people are perpetually falling from ladders and breaking an arm or a leg, until one night the chimney caught on fire. He was not seriously alarmed, but the roaring got louder and louder, and he was afraid that sparks from the blazing chimney might fall on the roof, and if he had to go up a ladder in the dark *he* might fall, so he put on his cape and rubbers and ran through the darkness calling for help.

The week before, a mountain lion had carried off a child, and the people of the village, horrified by this unheard-of accident, had dug a number of pits and covered them over with leaves and branches. Everyone in the village knew where they were and avoided walking on them, but because the old man never went out, nobody thought to tell him about the one that was two hundred yards from his house. Besides, it was in plain sight from his windows and he could have seen the men digging it, if only his curtains had not been drawn.

He lay at the bottom of the pit, sick with pain, and cried

for help, and at last he heard a child's voice somewhere above him saying, "Is that you?"

"I've hurt my back," the old man said. "You must go to the village and tell them to come at once and bring some ladders and lift me out. Tell them to bring ropes, too, that they can tie around their waists as they are descending the ladders, in case somebody falls."

There was no answer, and for a long time the old man thought the child had run to the village for help, and he lay there expecting the men to arrive with ropes and ladders and rescue him. Then, to his dismay, he heard the childish voice again, singing a little song, the words of which the child made up as he went along.

"Oh, please!" the old man said. "Whoever you are, stop singing and run to the village for help before it's too late."

"Too late for what?" asked the child.

"My back is hurt," the old man explained patiently, remembering how hard it is to capture the attention of children, and also trying to keep his language as plain as possible. "I walked on some leaves and the ground gave way and I fell in this pit and hurt my back, and if I have to lie here until morning, I'll die."

"It's never too late to die," the child said, and began singing again:

> "*Mercy, ride, my mare must know*
> *The holy tide, the turned-in toe*
> *They all must go . . .*"

"Go to the village," the old man said, "the place where all the houses are, and tell them—"

> "*Creep and hide,*" the child sang.
> "*The wall is down*

The scholar's pride, the satin gown
They all must drown . . ."

"Do as I say," the old man said, "and I'll give you a penny."

"Do you have it on you?" the child asked suspiciously.

"No," the old man said, "but I'll give it to you later."

"Promises don't interest me," the child said. "You're sure you haven't got a penny?"

"Go to the village or I'll tell your mother on you."

"I have no mother," said the child.

"I'll tell your father, then. Or don't you have any father, either?"

"No father," the child said. And then, *"No father, no bother; no murder, no matter; no wonder no thunder; no answer, no blunder; no—"*

"Stop," cried the old man. "Who are you, child? Have you no heart in your breast that you can see an old man dying in a pit and not run to the village for help?"

"I'm your heart's young cousin, Courage," said the child. "I'm keeping you company until you die."

For a long time there was silence and then the child said, "Are you still there?"

"Certainly," said the old man.

"I was afraid you'd gone," the child said.

"How can I," the old man said, weeping softly, "when I'm down at the bottom of a pit and my back is broken?"

"How can you be afraid of falling, then?" the child said.

"Am I really going to die?" the old man asked.

"Certainly."

"How soon?"

"Soon," said the child.

Then I don't think I am afraid any more," the old man said. "I don't know why. I just feel calm and safe."

"If you'd like me to," the child said, "I'll come down there and keep you company."

"You're not afraid of falling?"

"No," said the child. "I just let go."

"Let go," the old man repeated after him. "Let go," and he did, easily and happily and without a care in the world.

27

The man who had never been sick
a day in his life

ONCE upon a time there was a man who had never
been sick a day in his life. When other people were
doubled up with stomach cramps, or lay in a darkened
room waiting for a migraine to pass, or stuffed themselves
with pills that had no effect on their coughing and sneez-
ing, he was not unsympathetic, for he was a very kind
man, but the look in his eyes gave him away. It said all
too plainly that he didn't understand what pain and dis-
comfort were all about.

When his wife took sick, she filled a hot-water bottle
and made a collection on her bedside table of everything
she was likely to want, and when he came to the door and
said, with genuine concern in his voice, "Is there anything I
can do for you?" she said, "Yes, close the door and leave
me alone." So he did. A person who had ever been sick
might have felt guilty for being so well when his wife was
so miserable. All he felt was the kind of wonder people feel
at some flourish of human nature that defies understanding.

But the thing about perfection (and what he had was a kind of perfection) is that one minute it is there and the next it's gone, usually forever. And so the day came when the man who was never sick a day in his life was too sick to get up out of bed and lay in an upstairs room roaring like a bull. The hot-water bottle and the extra pillow behind his back and the nice appetizing tray with the best breakfast china on it he rejected indignantly. And when he couldn't give voice to his indignation because of the thermometer under his tongue, he glared balefully at his wife, as if his swollen glands and backache and hundred-and-one-and-two-tenths temperature were entirely her doing.

"Don't go spreading it all over the neighborhood," he said when she took the thermometer out of his mouth. But it was too remarkable an event to be kept from people, and in no time at all nice nourishing soups and calf's-foot jelly and even flowers began pouring into the house. At the sight of each new offering the man closed his eyes and said, "For God's sake, take it away. What can they be thinking of?"

"You," his wife said.

She left the soup or the calf's-foot jelly or whatever on the bedside table and went out of the room and stayed out a good long time. When she came back, the invalid's food was untouched, so she went right out again and stayed even longer. No remarks were made on either side, but there was a look in his eye that had never been there before, and it was not pleasure in being sick or gratefulness for small attentions. He wouldn't answer questions—wouldn't even speak. So she called the doctor, who was busy, like all doctors, and didn't come until she had given up hope of his ever coming. In the downstairs hall, as he was leaving, he repeated his instructions: the large pills to be given every four hours, the smaller pills at bedtime, with the capsules, and said that it would take time and to do what she could to make him comfortable.

"You don't know what you're saying," the woman said.

U PSTAIRS, the sick man heard their voices, which came quite plainly through the ceiling, and then—incredibly—the sound of suppressed laughter. The doctor was an old friend and the laughter was affectionate, but that didn't make any difference. In fact, it made it worse. A wave of hatred came over the man who had never been sick a day in his life—hatred not only of his wife and his friend but of life itself, which had lost its meaning and its virtue, and he realized that he had had enough of it and would just as soon not have any more. So he gave up, refused to lift a finger, stopped caring about anything, and with his face turned to the wall waited for the moment when they would realize that he had lost his hold on life and was going to die. He got well, of course. His body got well, in spite of everything, and rather sooner than his wife expected. His body got up out of bed and dressed and shaved and went to his office. There was a mountain of mail on his desk and the telephone was ringing. But it was a different man that answered it.

28

The woman who never drew breath
except to complain

IN a country near Finland dwelt a woman who never
drew breath except to complain. There was in that
country much to complain of—the long cold winters, the
scarcity of food, and robber bands that descended on
poor farmers at night and left their fields and barns
blazing. But these things the woman had by an inequality
of fate been spared. Her husband was young and strong
and worked hard and was kind to her. And they had
a child, a three-year-old boy, who was healthy and happy,
obedient and good. The roof never leaked, there was
always food in the larder and peat moss piled high outside
the door for the fireplace she cooked by. But still the
woman complained, morning, noon, and night.

One day when she was out feeding her hens, she heard a
great beating of wings and looked up anxiously, thinking it
was a hawk come to raid her hencoop, and saw a big white
gander, which sailed once around the house and then
settled at her feet and began to peck at the grain she had

scattered for her hens. While she was wondering how she could catch the wild bird without the help of her husband, who was away in the fields, it flapped its great soft wings and said, "So far as I can see, you have less than any woman in this country to complain about."

"That's true enough," the woman said.

"Then why do you do it?" asked the bird.

"Because there is so much injustice in the world," the woman said. "In the village yesterday a woman in her sleep rolled over on her child and smothered it, and an old man starved to death last month, within three miles of here. Wherever I look, I see human misery, and here there is none, and I am afraid."

"Of what?" asked the bird.

"I am afraid lest they look down from the sky and see how blessed I am, compared to my neighbors, and decide to even things up a bit. This way, if they do look down, they will also hear me complaining, and think, 'That poor woman has lots to contend with,' and go on about their business."

"Very clever of you," the bird said, cleaning the underside of its wing with its beak. "But in the sky anything but the truth has a hollow ring. One more word of complaint out of you and all the misfortunes of all your neighbors will be visited on you and on your husband and child." The bird flapped its wings slowly, rose above her, sailed once around the chimney, and then, flying higher and higher, was lost in the clouds. While the woman stood peering after it, the bread that she had left in the oven burned to a cinder.

THE bread was the beginning of many small misfortunes, which occurred more and more frequently as time went on. The horse went lame, the hens stopped laying, and after too long a season of rain the hay all rotted in the fields. The cow went dry but produced no calf. The roof began to leak, and when the woman's husband went up to fix it, he fell and broke his leg and was laid up for months, with winter coming on. And while the woman was outside, trying to do his work for him, the child pulled a kettle of boiling water off the stove and was badly scalded.

And still no word of complaint crossed the woman's lips. In her heart she knew that worse things could happen, and in time worse things did. A day came when there was nothing to eat in the larder and the woman had to go the rounds of her neighbors and beg for food, and those she had never turned hungry from her door refused her, on the ground that anyone so continually visited by misfortune must at some time have had sexual intercourse with the Devil. The man's leg did not heal, and the child grew sickly and pale. The woman searched for edible roots and berries, and set snares for rabbits and small birds, and so kept her family from starving, until one day, when she was far away in the marshes, some drunken soldiers happened by and wantonly set fire to the barns, and went on their way, reeling and tittering. The heat of the burning barns made a downdraft, and a shower of sparks landed on the thatched roof of the farmhouse, and that, too, caught on fire. In a very few minutes, while the neighbors stood around in a big circle, not daring to come nearer because of the heat of the flames, the house burned to the ground, and the man and the child both perished. When the woman came running across the fields, crying and wringing her hands, people who had known her all their lives and were moved at last by her misfortunes tried to intercept her and lead her away, but she would have none of them. At nightfall they left her there, and she did not even see them go. She sat with her head on her knees and listened for the sound of wings.

At midnight the great bird sailed once around the blackened chimney and settled on the ground before her, its feathers rosy with the glow from the embers. The bird seemed to be waiting for her to speak, and when she said nothing it stretched its neck and arched its back and finally said, in a voice much kinder than the last time, "This is a great pity. All the misfortunes of all your neighbors have been visited on you, without a word of complaint from you to bring them on. But the gods can't be everywhere at once, you know, and sometimes they get the cart before the horse. If you'd like to complain now, you may." The wind blew a shower of sparks upward and the bird fanned them away with its wings. The woman did not speak. "This much I can do for you," the bird said, "and I wish it was more."

When the woman raised her head, she saw a young man whose face, even in the dying firelight, she recognized. There before her stood her child, her little son, but grown now, in the pride of manhood. All power of speech left her. She put out her arms and in that instant, brought on by such a violent beating of wings as few men have ever dreamed of, the air turned white. What the woman at first took to be tiny feathers proved to be snow. It melted against her cheek, and turned her hair white, and soon put the fire out.

The snow came down all night, and all the next day, and

for many days thereafter, and was so deep that it lasted all winter, and in the spring grass grew up in what had once been the rooms of the farmhouse, but of the woman there was no trace whatever.

29

The old man at the railroad crossing

"Rejoice," said the old man at the railroad crossing, to every person who came that way. He was very old, and his life had been full of troubles, but he was still able to lower the gates when a train was expected, and raise them again when it had passed by in a whirl of dust and diminishing noise. It was just a matter of time before he would be not only old but bedridden, and so, meanwhile, people were patient with him and excused his habit of saying "Rejoice," on the ground that when you are that old not enough oxygen gets to the brain.

But it was curious how differently different people reacted to that one remark. Those who were bent on accumulating money, or entertaining dreams of power, or just busy, didn't even hear it. The watchman was somebody who was supposed to guard the railroad crossing, not to tell people how they ought to feel, and if there had been such a thing as a wooden or mechanical watchman, they would have been just as satisfied.

Those who cared about good manners were embarrassed for the poor old fellow, and thought it kinder to ignore his affliction.

And those who were really kind, but not old, and not

particularly well acquainted with trouble, said "Thank you" politely, and passed on, without in the least having understood what he meant. Or perhaps it was merely that they were convinced he didn't mean anything, since he said the same thing day in and day out, regardless of the occasion or who he said it to. "Rejoice," he said solemnly, looking into their faces. "Rejoice."

The children, of course, were not embarrassed, and did not attempt to be kind. They snickered and said, "Why?" and got no answer, and so they asked another question: "Are you crazy?" And—as so often happened when they asked a question they really wanted to know the answer to—he put his hand on their head and smiled, and they were none the wiser.

But one day a woman came along, a nice-looking woman with gray hair and lines in her face and no interest in power or money or politeness that was merely politeness and didn't come from the heart, and no desire to be kind for the sake of being kind, either, and when the old man said "Rejoice," she stopped and looked at him thoughtfully and then she said, "I don't know what at." But not crossly. It was just a statement.

When the train had gone by and the old man had raised the gates, instead of walking on like the others, she stood there, as if she had something more to say and didn't know how to say it. Finally she said, "This has been the worst year and a half of my entire life. I think I'm getting through it, finally. But it's been very hard."

"Rejoice," the old man said.

"Even so?" the woman asked. And then she said, "Well, perhaps you're right. I'll try. You've given me something to think about. Thank you very much." And she went on down the road.

ONE morning shortly after this, there was a new watchman at the crossing, a smart-looking young man
who tipped his hat to those who had accumulated power or
money, and bowed politely to those who valued good
manners, and thanked the kind for their kindness, and to
the children he said, "If you hang around my crossing,
you'll wish you hadn't." So they all liked him, and felt that
there had been a change for the better. What had happened
was that the old man couldn't get up out of bed. Though
he felt just as well as before, there was no strength in his
legs. So there he lay, having to be fed and shaved and
turned over in bed and cared for like a baby. He lived with
his daughter, who was a slatternly housekeeper and had
more children than she could care for and a husband who
drank and beat her, and the one thing that had made her
life possible was that her old father was out of the house all
day, watching the railroad crossing. So when she brought
him some gruel for his breakfast that morning and he said
"Rejoice," she set her mouth in a grim line and said nothing. When she brought him some more of the same gruel
for his lunch she was ready to deal with the situation.
Standing over him, so that she seemed very tall, she said,
"Father, I don't want to hear that word again. If you can't
say anything but 'Rejoice,' don't say anything, do you
hear?" And she thought he seemed to understand. But
when she brought him his supper, he said it again, and in
her fury she slapped him. Her own father. The tears rolled
down his furrowed cheeks into his beard, and they looked
at each other as they hadn't looked at each other since he
was a young man and she was a little girl skipping along at
his side. For a moment, her heart melted, but then she

thought of how hard her life was, and that he was making it even harder by living on like this when it was time for him to die. And so she turned and went out of the room, without saying that she was sorry. And after that the old man avoided her eyes and said nothing whatever.

One day she put her head in the door and said, "There's somebody to see you."

It was the gray-haired woman. "I heard you were not feeling up to par," she said, and when the old man didn't say anything, she went on, "I made this soup for my family, and I thought you might like some. It's very nourishing." She looked around and saw that the old man's daughter had left them, so she sat down on the edge of the bed and fed the soup to him. She could tell by the way he ate it, and the way the color came into his face, that he was hungry. The dark little room looked as if it hadn't been swept in a month of Sundays, but she knew better than to start cleaning another woman's house. She contented herself with tucking the sheets in properly and straightening the covers and adjusting the pillow behind the old man's head—for which he seemed grateful, though he didn't say anything.

"Now I must go," she said. But she didn't go. Instead she looked at him and said, "Things aren't any better, they're worse. Much worse. I really don't know what I'm going to do." And when he didn't say what she expected him to say, she stopped thinking about herself and thought about him. "I don't care for the new watchman at the crossing," she said. "He stands talking to the girls when he ought to be letting the gates down, and I'm afraid some child will be run over."

But this seemed to be of no interest to him, and she quickly saw why. Death was what was on his mind, not the railroad crossing. His own death, and how to meet it. And she saw that he was feeling terribly alone.

She took his frail old hand in hers and said, "If I can just get through this day, maybe things will be better tomorrow, but in any case, I'll come to see you, to see how you are." And then, without knowing that she was going to say it but only thinking that he didn't have much longer to wait, she said what he used to say at the railroad crossing, to every person who came that way.

A   NOTE   ON   THE   TYPE

THE text of this book was set on the Linotype in Janson, a recutting made direct from type cast from matrices long thought to have been made by the Dutchman Anton Janson, who was a practicing type founder in Leipzig during the years 1668–87. However, it has been conclusively demonstrated that these types are actually the work of Nicholas Kis (1650–1702), a Hungarian, who most probably learned his trade from the master Dutch type founder Dirk Voskens. The type is an excellent example of the influential and sturdy Dutch types that prevailed in England up to the time William Caslon developed his own incomparable designs from these Dutch faces.